JACKS

STEVIE,
GET IT
GIRL!
N

JACKS

Betting on Love #2

NAOMI SPRINGTHORP

Jacks, Betting on Love #2

Copyright © 2020 Love & Devotion Author Services, Inc.

Published by Love & Devotion Author Services, Inc.

Print Edition ISBN 978-1-949243-19-2

Jacks is a work of fiction and does not in any way advocate irresponsible behavior. This book contains content that is not suitable for readers 17 and under. Please store your files where they cannot be accessed by minors. Any resemblance to actual things, events, locales, or persons living or dead is entirely coincidental. Names, characters, places, brands, products, media, and incidents are either the product of the author's imagination or are used fictitiously. The author acknowledges the trademark status and ownership of any location names or products mentioned in this book. The author received no compensation for any mention of said trademark.

Cover Photo: Tonya Clark All About the Covers

Graphic Designer: Irene Johnson johnsoni@mac.com

Editor: Katrina Fair

Never give up on your dreams.

Make the bet.

Take the risk.

CHAPTER ONE

My life has been crazy. So, let me get you caught up. My four-day weekend in Las Vegas for auditions was so much more than I expected it to be. I had no idea it was going to change my whole world.

I don't know where to start.

I managed to get to all six of my auditions. You already know I got a call back on my Stardust Supper Club audition. The Supper Club people called and offered me two sets every Saturday night. They were clear that they want to give me more, but I need to earn it because I don't have the experience they're looking for.

I had two auditions at the MGM. The first to be a cast member for their EFX production, but they require dance skills that I simply don't have. The second was for a female voice to add to a lounge show featuring rock music, that's all the information I had walking in—they didn't provide any other notes or song requirements. You can imagine my surprise when the guy doing the auditions was no other than Mr. Obnoxious himself. His exact words were, "I want someone to compliment me baby, not upstage me. I have an idea for something else I'd like to do with you though. I know men would love to see you and that hot ass on stage. I'll call you." I didn't take him seriously. I mean he's all schtick all the time and if he calls me, well he's probably after a piece of ass and I'm not doing that even if it gets me a gig.

I didn't pull off country good enough for the audition I had at Treasure Island. They said I wasn't believable as a country artist and I should stick to rock/pop. Honestly, that suits me fine.

I walked before my turn to audition came up at Circus Circus. I watched them put costumes on artists and expect them to tell stupid jokes, among other things—not my scene.

Lastly, I auditioned to be a member of a lounge band at Caesar's Palace. The audition went well and I got a call back that I had to call in sick and banzai run to Vegas for. But, I haven't got a second call back.

I accepted the offer from the Stardust, it's a step in the right direction. At least the two sets will cover the cost of my gas and the night they want me is Saturday, so it won't have any effect on my day job. They asked me to put together a set list and submit it to them in the next week. They'll be scheduling individual practices and a complete run-through in a few weeks. Needless to say, I find myself wandering the stacks in the warehouse and watching for songs to jump out at me.

Then there's Danny. The only man that deserves me. The biggest mistake I've ever made. My British lie to find out he prefers California Girls—it was a bit too late. The only time I can remember not having the strength to tell the truth because my heart couldn't take the possibility of losing him and the only time I've ever been afraid. The only man that makes me do crazy shit. My happy. I believed we'd never be together again. I'd never talk to him again. He was gone, and it was over. I assumed that he'd married another woman, knowing with all of my heart and soul that he loves me and not her. My heart was functioning cardiovascularly, but there would never again be any thought of the L word. Seeing him again, meeting his daughter, talking with him, spending the night with him alone, laughing with him, feeling his touch and simply being with him. Learning that he didn't marry her and that he still loves me. He wants to be with me and is going to find a way. It'll take time and I may need to be a secret for a while. I'm okay with that.

Wow, he still loves me. I haven't said the L word. I've totally fallen for him, but I need to be sure this is real and he isn't going to be gone again. I couldn't take losing him again. I want to make him happy and be with him. We have the same heat, attraction, and emotions for each other after so long, we never let go of each other. I'm not letting go now. I'm never going to lose him again.

Now that I'll be in Las Vegas every weekend, I'll at least get to see Danny even if we can't spend time together. The chef for the Supper Club hasn't been announced yet, the top three have submitted their menus and are waiting for the next step.

Danny told *her* that he wants to start going out again. It didn't go over well. Once she realized he didn't want to go out with her, she flipped out. She asked him why and he simply told her that he wanted to be happy, not miserable. She's been leaving him with more than his share of Jackie duty, and disappearing for two days at a time without notice and with no regard for his work schedule or hers. Doing her best to make it as hard as possible for him to date again. He's been calling me from pay phones when he can, not wanting to make it any worse. Luckily, she isn't working at the same place anymore, so he's been able to call me when he has breaks at work, and she isn't there watching him. It's a bad situation. When I hear his voice it makes me happy and the longer we talk the more happy I hear in him. He tells me everything about Jackie and about work. He gives me updates on the chef position at the Supper Club, and he's proud of me for getting the gig, even if it's only one night a week. Proud of me and tells me so. He says it's only the beginning. He also tells me how much he misses me and how happy he is to have me back in his life, and of course some dirty stuff about what he'd like to do with me.

Bryan, isn't so happy. He doesn't like that I'll be spending every weekend in Vegas and therefore missing his gigs. But, so far he hasn't put the smile on my face together with Danny being back, he thinks it's the fact that I got the job. Now that I think about it, I'm a little ticked at Bryan for not supporting me and being selfish about this. It doesn't matter, he's not Danny. He didn't even want to talk about my set list. Stupid boy, can't simply be a friend.

I've been trying to focus on my set list. The director asked for a long set list, so they can make adjustments for any over-lapping or inappropriate song choices. I'm including my tryout song "Get Here," something from Bonnie Raitt, possibly the new Firehouse ballad. I want to make an impact with my song choices and I'd like to arrange a few of my favorites into a more Supper Club style. It shouldn't be a problem since there will be a live house band.

While the real world continues on around me, I find it hard to escape my personal bubble. I've worked hard and put so much effort into my singing, this chance is what I've been waiting for. The fact that Danny is there with me, well there's only so much a girl can take and remain capable of handling her day to day life.

One night after work, I was sitting at home finalizing my set list for the Supper Club, when the phone rang and the caller ID showed a 702 number. I picked up immediately, excited to talk to Danny, "Hey baby!"

"Well, I love that sweetheart. How'd you know it was me?"

A deeper voice that was not my Danny. "Or, do you always answer the phone that way? Is this Jackie?"

"Sorry. Yes, this is Jackie." What the fuck was I thinking!

"Great! I told you I would call, so I'm calling. This is Ron. You auditioned for me at the MGM."

Crap! It's Mr. Obnoxious! "Oh, yeah. Um, hi."

"So, I'd like to get together with you. I've got some ideas of things we could do together."

Creep. "I'm not interested. Thanks."

"Really? Then why'd you audition?"

"I'm looking for a gig, not a date," came flying out in the bitchiest tone ever.

"I knew it. I like you. When can I meet with you?"

"I'll be performing at the new Supper Club at the Stardust on Saturday nights."

"Even better. I'll be in touch," and he hung up.

What the hell just happened? Is Mr. Obnoxious stalking me? Whatever. Not important. My set list is priority one. That is until the phone rings, "Hello?" sounding a bit put out.

"Hey Jacks, how was your day, baby?" Danny's voice makes my heart beat faster and my cheeks hurt from grinning.

"Hey babe! I've been thinking about you."

"I miss you, Jacks. Do you know when you're coming back to Vegas?" His voice low and tender.

"Soon. I'm expecting the Supper Club practice to start the end of next week. I miss you too, Danny."

"I need you, baby. I don't want to lose you again." Then he was gone, too many people in the break room on a short break.

Back to my set list. I've got my list ready to go and I'm hoping I have enough. Something like this:

1. "Get Here" by Oleta Adams
2. "I Can't Make You Love Me" by Bonnie Raitt
3. "Stay" by Lisa Loeb
4. Beatles Medley ("Here Comes the Sun"/"Black-bird"/"Golden Slumbers"/"Dear Prudence"/"I Will"/"If I Fell"/"And I Love Her"/"In My Life")
5. "Black Velvet" by Alannah Myles
6. "What About Me" by Moving Pictures
7. "Come To My Window" by Melissa Etheridge
8. "Long December" by Counting Crows
9. "I Don't Want To Miss a Thing" by Aerosmith
10. "What I Am" by Edie Brickell and the New Bohemians
11. "Beautiful In My Eyes" by Joshua Kadison
12. "I Live My Life For You" by Firehouse
13. "Show Me the Way" by Styx
14. "High Enough" by Damn Yankees
15. "Into the Night" by Benny Mardones
16. "To Be With You" by Mr. Big
17. "I Remember You" by Skid Row

Yes, that's it! I'm happy with that list! I email it to the Supper Club people and check my email to find they've sent me scheduling details. I'm scheduled for costume fitting and individual run-through next Saturday, then a full dress rehearsal on Sunday. We open the following weekend.

I can't believe this is happening! I have so much to do! I need to... and I stop myself because I can't call Danny and share my excitement with him. I pick up the phone to call Dot and share the news, when there's a knock on my door and Bryan lets himself in. I quickly finish my phone call and hang up.

"So, back to Vegas next weekend for your gig?" he asks with no enthusiasm at all.

"Just a practice and dress rehearsal next weekend. We open the following weekend." I can't contain myself. I'm bubbling over like a bottle of champagne that got shook before the cork popped!

"Cool. Where are you staying?"

Crap! I knew I was forgetting something. "Don't know yet. I need to work on that. I'm hoping I can crash with someone from the show on Saturday night and drive home Sunday, but no idea for next weekend." I wonder if I can get a room at the Stardust.

"Supper Club at the Stardust, right?" Bryan has been listening.

Crap. "Yes."

"Cool. You'll be great." Then he sits down with his guitar and starts playing the songs he knows off my set list. No commentary on song choices. Not singing. "Are you going to sing with me or what?" He finally calls me over.

I can't resist and I need all the practice that I can get. Some of the songs I chose for my list, well I've never sung them outside of the shower.

CHAPTER TWO

I finally get to tell Danny about the show schedule and I love how he gets excited with me. He's beaming with pride and adoration. He's serving his menu to the production team this Friday and the chef is supposed to be announced this weekend.

"Jacks, I hope I get to see you this weekend. But, you know it might not happen unless I have Jackie with me or it might only be while I'm at work. Just know that I want more than that and I'll do what I can to make it happen."

"I understand, baby. I'll be there every weekend now, so I'll never be that far off. You do what you need to do. I'm your secret, Danny—nobody else's."

"Soon baby, you won't be a secret. Can't wait to see you this weekend," and he was gone again when the voices around him in the break room started getting loud.

Thursday morning before practice weekend, I'm woken up by a phone call. "Hello?" I answer sleepily.

"Hi, is Jackie available? This is Katy from the Supper Club." A very fun and feminine sounding voice comes through with a presence.

"Good morning. This is Jackie."

"Great! I emailed you yesterday and haven't received a response. They want you here for all of the individual practices and the dress rehearsal. The guys think you have the best grasp on the music they're looking for. Anyway, they want you at the Supper Club for breakfast Friday morning 8am."

"I need to get the time off from my other job, it shouldn't be a problem. Can I call you back in an hour?"

"Sure. I get it. Short notice, expecting you to be here tomorrow morning."

Shit! I need to leave tonight after work! "Katy, I need to find a place to stay while I'm in Vegas. Do you happen to know anybody with a couch I can crash on?"

"I can probably get the guys to get you a room at the hotel for this weekend since you're coming in early and doing extra duty. Talk to me when you get here."

"Awesome, I'll call you back soon to confirm. Appreciate you, Katy."

"No worries," and she hangs up.

I get my ass out of bed and to work as quickly as possible. Walking into my boss's office 15 minutes before I'm scheduled to be at work and he glares at me like, 'what now?'

"Hey, Joe. Do you have a minute?"

"What's up?" he asks without looking up.

"I've been auditioning for singing gigs and I got one in Vegas, but it's only one night a week and it's Saturday. So, I didn't think it would be a problem and I still don't. But, we open next weekend and they need me there tomorrow morning through Sunday this weekend to help with the music, instead of Saturday and Sunday for my practice and dress rehearsal. I just got the call this morning. Is there any way I can get tomorrow off? Please."

"What's your gig?" Still not looking up from his paperwork.

"The Stardust is opening a Supper Club. It's going to have great food and dancing with live music. I'll be singing two sets on Saturday nights."

"Can you get me a pair of tickets for opening night?"

"I can try, let me make a call." I walk over to my desk and dial Katy.

"Hello?"

"Hey Katy, this is Jackie. My boss says I can leave if I get him a pair of tickets to opening night. So, how much are they?" I figure I can buy him the tickets.

"Well, the guys changed their mind and they want you here like now. They actually said yesterday, but 6pm tonight will work. Since you'll be here for tasting tomorrow, they want you here for all of the tastings and the first one is tonight. Tell your boss you can get him four tickets that include dinner and two drinks each, if you can be here before 6pm today." Holy crap! This is absolutely crazy!

"Katy, is this going to keep happening or is this a one time thing for me to need to be there during the week?" I ask, not sure I want the answer.

"I have no idea. Make yourself valuable and they'll make the times they want you fit your schedule, or pay you enough so you don't need to work anywhere else."

"Yes, ma'am! I'll call you right back." I hang up and head back to Joe's office.

"Joe." He finally looks up from his desk to find me buzzing with excitement.

"You get tickets?"

"Yes, but I have a counter offer."

He stops what he's doing and leans back in his chair. "I'm listening."

"Four tickets to opening night including dinner and two drinks each, if I can leave at lunch today. They want me there before 6pm today now. Please. I'm really sorry for the short notice. Please Joe." I'm almost begging.

He takes a deep breath, "Sing part of the song you did to try out for me."

I stop and stare at him funny. Joe has always been a cool guy and put up with me, but he never asked about me. I take a deep breath and start singing "Get Here" a cappella.

Joe smiles and stops me, "Tell them I need a table for eight and I'll pay for the extra four. Now, get out of here and make me proud, kid."

I run behind his desk and hug him tight before I take off like a shot to go home and pack for Vegas.

I call Katy and let her know I'm on my way and that Joe needs a table for eight. Since I'm going to be there the whole weekend at their request, the guys got me my own room at the Stardust. I check in with Dot, so she's aware the plan has changed. I need to tell Danny, but I don't have a way to reach him. I don't want to surprise him when he walks in to serve his menu. I try the no-tell motel number thinking that maybe Tony still lives there…

"Hello?"

"Tony?"

"Yes."

Yay! "Tony, this is Jackie. Are you going to talk to Danny soon?"

"Jackie? You mean, Danny's Jacks?" The confusion in his voice makes me wonder if maybe I'm more of a secret than I realized.

"Um, maybe." Shit.

"Hold on." I hear him passing the phone to someone else.

"Hello?" Danny's voice comes through clear.

"Hi, baby." Not sure what to say.

"Hey Jacks! Why are you calling here?"

"I don't have a number that I can call you at and I don't

want you to be caught off guard because my Supper Club schedule changed. I'm now included in the menu tastings." I scream in joy at the thought of trying his food and raving over it, to help get him the chef gig—even though I'm sure he'll be named chef either way.

"Really?"

"Yes! And, I'm getting in my truck to drive there as soon as I hang up the phone. They want me there for all of the practices. They want me to help with the music. I need to be there for the first tasting tonight at 6pm." I'm so fucking excited that I can hardly maintain myself.

"Jacks! That's awesome. They want you more involved. That's a good sign. Even better, I'll get to see you sooner." He says with a selfish, dirty tone.

"And since I'm going early at their request, they got me a room right there at the Stardust for the whole weekend."

"That's convenient. Maybe I can come visit you." I can hear his dirty grin and it makes my insides flip around like a kid on a trampoline.

"Um, did I blow it calling Tony? I didn't even think that I might be a secret from him." Hoping I didn't cause a huge problem.

"No babe, you don't worry about that. Tony has my back. He knew I saw you as soon as he saw the smile on my face. I'm working room service until 11pm tonight, so call and order once you get to your room. Don't worry if you don't get back in time, this is a big deal for you and you need to see it through. Rock 'em Jacks!"

"You're fucking amazing. I can't wait until I can rock you again, Danny," I say in my sexiest voice.

"Tony didn't need to see my hard-on. Can't wait to see you, babe. Drive safe," and he hangs up.

I toss every conceivable thing that I might need into my bag and hit the road.

CHAPTER THREE

Non-stop trip to Vegas, midweek, and during the day with no traffic. My best time yet, I made the drive in under three hours. I walk into the Supper Club and find Katy.

"You're early!"

"No traffic. Do I have time to go to my room and freshen up?"

"Yes, but the guys want you here at 5pm now. It's always something with them. Here's your room key."

"Thanks! Dress code for tonight?"

"Not really. Be you, but better than your driving clothes." She looks me up and down, judging my holey jeans and heavy metal T-shirt.

"I never changed after I got ready for work, sorry about that."

"That's work clothes? Where do you work?"

I laugh, "I work in a music warehouse doing phone sales. My job is to know the music and help stores have the right selection on hand, including special order stuff they have a hard time keeping in stock."

"Huh. You really do know music and that's why the guys

want you here. They need you because they know what they like, but that's about it."

"Good to know." I check the time and take off for my room as quickly as I can before anybody else spots me. However I don't succeed, Danny catches me running to the elevator as he's walking through the lobby. He runs and catches up with me, making it on the elevator before the doors close.

"Hey baby!" He grabs me, holding me tight to him and burying his face in my hair. "Allow me to escort you to your room."

I'm horrible. I don't speak. I entangle my fingers in his hair and pull him down to me, kissing him like I'm an addict and he's my drug. My open mouth on his lips, he slides his tongue in my mouth and everything else disappears. Can I have him now, please?

We get to the seventh floor and I follow him to my room, 721. Danny follows me into the room and I give him the second key in case he wants to come in later or any time this weekend.

"I gotta go. I'm on the clock and can't go missing." Danny says and walks toward the door.

"Okay. I have to get ready and be at the Supper Club by 5pm. So, I'll just be here naked in the shower for the next little bit." I'm evil.

Danny stares at me, the heat emanating from him, "Jacks, you're killing me."

I start to strip and turn on the shower. Danny reaches for my naked body, needing me. "I'll be here for you later, Danny. We both need to work. We can't screw this up."

"I know. Tonight, Jacks," and he was gone.

Exactly what I needed to boost my confidence for the Supper Club guys and to light up my smile.

I move into the room, getting all of my things where I want them and my clothes hung up. The shower is steaming up the bathroom, so I tie my hair up in a knot and take a few minutes to relax with the hot water beating down on my neck and shoulders. I close my eyes and all I can see is Danny happier than I've ever seen him, he's holding my hand with Jackie riding on his shoulders. The sense of happiness and hope that runs through me tells me I'm doing the right thing, and pushes me forward. I need to be in Las Vegas. I'm getting my happy.

I tune the radio to the hard rock station and turn up the volume, so I can get in the mood while I get ready for Supper Club time. Huh. Maybe I should be listening to different music. Metal isn't really the Supper Club style. But, it does get me pumped up. I need a CD with my Supper Club Set on it, I guess I need to work on that once I have my final set list. I keep thinking about the music while I thumb through the clothes I brought, trying to decide what to wear. I want to make a good impression and I want them to take me seriously, both while being me. I pull on my tight, faded black jeans and my black suede boots, folding them down to make them knee height. I slide my sleeveless black draped top over my head and wish I had more accessories as I examine the low neckline, a long necklace would be perfect. I realize that I may need to go shopping if I'm going to make it through the weekend without wearing the same clothes. I untie my hair and shake it down to see what I'm working with, and the knot left me with a touch of wave that will be perfect for tonight. I put my make-up on, without going overboard because I'm in Vegas, shove my room key, ID and money in my pocket and head out the door.

I get to the Supper Club early, which is what I wanted and search for Katy. There's no one to be seen, so I call out, "Katy."

"SShhhhh…." I hear as Katy comes walking out from behind a curtain. "Oh, perfect. You're here. I need to introduce you to the guys."

"Wait, am I acceptable for the dress code? I don't want to screw this up."

"You're fine, and funny. Don't worry about it." Katy reassures me. "Children! Come out here, please." She calls out.

I'm completely lost and worried that I'm the new babysitter, when I watch them walk out. All of them.

"Hey everybody, this is Jackie. The guys had me bring her in early to help with music, so she's joining the team for this weekend and will also be performing on Saturday nights. I anticipate her role here to change over the next few weeks. She's new. Be nice to her. Only light hazing."

I turn to Katy somewhat unsure of the situation and admire the way she takes control.

Continuing with introductions, "These three ladies will be helping with styling you and dressing you. This is George, she's the style guru and final approval before you walk on stage."

"Katy, stop! You know I love it when you remember I'm a girl at heart!" George shines, "Fabulous to meet you, Miss Thing!"

"This is Maria and Robyn, they're designers and seamstresses. The team of them will help you with accessories and all that," Katy says as she looks me up and down realizing I have no accessories and I'm wearing only black.

"This is Marni, love her and treat her right because she does hair and make-up—and you'll never want to do your own again when you see what she does!" Katy gushes.

"Flattery will get you everywhere with me, nice to meet you," Marni reaches out and shakes my hand, as she rolls her eyes at Katy.

"The group of nerds over there is our stage crew and you'll get to know them. They change up a bit depending on the day. They take no offense to being referred to as whatever job they're doing that day. Lights, Curtains, Sound, you get the idea. As long as you do it nicely."

As a group they silently wave at me and I return the gesture. They seem a bit like a group of shy children, or maybe it's the nerdy inexperience with women and my low cut top.

"I basically run everything and do everything else. These guys think they do, but they would be lost without me and I make things happen. These two are the guys with the titles, but we refer to them as the guys since they pretty much do it all together. This is Smith and Wesson."

The whole room laughs. "I'm sorry. This is James Smith and Kyle Karrs. I just like to point out the guns they're sporting." Katy gets a huge grin on her face and I look the guys over.

James is tall, slender and has a head full of dirty blonde curly hair that has a mind of its own. He's wearing overpriced jeans and an untucked plaid button up shirt with short sleeves that look too short for his long torso. He has clear blue eyes and a friendly smile. His arms are toned, but not anywhere near guns.

Kyle is average height, a couple inches shorter than James and has dark short, almost buzzed hair. He's average build, if not slightly on the heavy side, and wearing olive drab cargo pants with a black T-shirt and the matching olive drab flack jacket. His hazel eyes shine with an interesting light, like there's always something sparking. The only guns I envision him having are plastic and make a machine-gun noise when you pull on the trigger or possibly shoot water.

I go to each of them individually and shake their hands. "I'm so happy to be here. Thank you for giving me a shot at this. I really appreciate it."

They both look at me and then each other, "We think you have a better idea of what we want for music at the Supper

Club than we do," Kyle speaks for both of them. I can't contain my smile.

"Alright already! Enough of the make-out session. The band is backstage and they've been working on songs from the set lists. Sound wants to dial it in a bit with the full band and vocals. You can help with that and entertain us before we sit down to dinner and try chef #1's menu." Katy directs me to the stage and I'm ecstatic!

"Yes, ma'am!"

I walk backstage to find the band tuning instruments and setting up drums. I introduce myself and they knew I was coming. It was 'nice to meet you Jackie' coming from all directions along with high fives and fist bumps. I love it!

"Let's do this, guys!"

"You know it, Jackie. We've got some things worked up for you. So, we're going to put you on the spot and see what happens." A bald man in his mid-thirties seems to be the voice for the band.

"I'm in. Curtains!" I call out wanting the stage to be open and get this thing moving. "Are we rockin' this or sticking to Supper Club?"

The band smiles at me and the leader says, "Tell us what you think of this medley. I'll give you a queue when we're changing songs. 1, 2, 3, 4!" and the music goes.

Beatles! Couldn't be better to start with! They put together my medley, rearranged the song order, added "Two Of Us" and left "In My Life" for last. A-fricking-mazing! Perfect changeovers from song to song, no stumbling or awkwardness seaming the songs together. We finish the medley and I can't contain my excitement, I clap and cheer! Then the rest of the team listening does the same. I turn to the band, "You guys are tight!" The band hazed me from then until the chef walked in to serve his menu, playing songs and making me sing without even a clue of what they were going to play. Overall, I did pretty good.

When the chef walked in, the band and I joined the rest of the team for dinner, but Kyle called me over to sit with him and James. Katy introduced the chef, "This is our tasting of chef #1's menu. Each of you have a card for rating each of the dishes and noting any comments you might have. Feel free to ask the chef questions." Then Katy sat with me and the guys.

"Hi, I'm Chef Francois." He's an older man with a low timbre to his voice and a French accent. "I imagine a French inspired Supper Club, with a menu featuring fresh ingredients and tasty sauces. I've been asked to serve my menu tapas style, so each of you can get a couple of bites of everything. To start, you're being served a shooter of my Fresh Pea Soup, Escargot with my special roasted garlic and my Fig and Olive Tapenade with Brie." He lost me at escargot, I'm not touching it! "There will of course be a soup of the day option and green salad option available. Next, is my Tarragon Chicken with mushrooms and lemon cream sauce, and my Rosemary Roasted Turkey with baby potatoes and my Cassoulet—all will be main course options. For dessert, I offer seasonal flavored Creme Brûlée, Apple Tarte Tatin, and a sampler plate with French Meringues, Bite-sized Cream Puffs, Madeleines and Macaroons that will be served with a chocolate sauce and a raspberry compote. Please enjoy."

Katy stands up, "Does anybody have any questions?" She surveys the room and it's silent.

She obviously needs someone to ask him a question, so I chime in, "You've given us samples of almost everything, but only one of the desserts. Why not the Apple Tart and the sampler? Also, is there any bread with your menu? Some of these items are very tasty." Katy gives me a nod of appreciation.

Chef Francois answers uncomfortably, "Bread fills you up,

not allowing you to eat all of my food. Creme Brûlée is a dessert favorite and I decided to give each of you a normal size serving of that instead of a sample of each dessert."

"Thank you, Chef Francois. You may go." Katy stands and Chef leaves the room. "Okay, everybody take a minute and fill out the card or write down your opinion. Eat everything that you want and leave what you don't like. Don't worry about being polite."

Everybody finished eating and nobody touched the escargot. Half of the pea soup was still sitting on the table and the entrees were all tasted, but very few finished. Honestly, he lost me at escargot and I couldn't put anything else in my mouth without thinking slugs! The dessert sounded delicious, but then he served a sauce that tasted almost burnt with it and needless to say I'll be getting a pizza later.

Katy studied me observing and asked, "What are you looking at?"

"Just noticing how much of the food is left on the plates untouched or only tasted. As a group, are we the clientele that the show will be entertaining and feeding?" I'm thinking to myself that Danny has this in the bag.

"Interesting observation." She got up and went after the guys.

The band pulled me back on stage and sound was directing us, trying to get everything set up for the practices that start in the morning. Then Katy and the guys came back.

"Jackie, do you want to go through your individual practice tonight so we have that out of the way and you can get your set list locked in first? Then the ladies can work on your wardrobe and have things pulled for you to try when we have some time tomorrow," Katy taking care of business for the guys.

"Whatever you want to do is great." I'll be agreeable to the end.

"Great, let's do this. No need to go over the Beatles

Medley, we all loved that." Katy and the guys get comfortable and call out the songs they want to hear until we have gone through most of them.

About an hour and a half later, I'm hyped up and we have ran through all the songs on my set list except the Beatles Medley and "Get Here," which are definitely in my set.

"The guys want to go over their notes together and get back to you tomorrow with your firm list. Robyn would like you to visit her real quick, so she can get some measurements. The guys want you here for breakfast at 10am tomorrow morning. Check with me before you leave for the night. Thank you and great job." Katy does everything. Maybe she's telepathic or something. I rarely hear the guys actually speak.

I find Robyn and let her take my measurements, which only takes her a few minutes. Though I have to say that I had no idea how many measurements she would take. I mean the places she measured, I could be getting a custom skintight leather jumpsuit.

I find Katy before I go out in search of pizza, "Hey, you wanted to see me?"

"Yes, the guys are impressed with you—your singing, your song choices, your insight on the food, and your backbone. So am I. What are your plans tonight?" Katy asked.

"I was thinking about finding a pizza and then relaxing in my room with a movie. I want to be fresh tomorrow."

"Sounds like a plan. I know a great pizza place, join me. Then get some rest and be ready to party tomorrow night because we're going out."

"I'm in!" and we leave the building.

CHAPTER FOUR

Katy leads me out the front door of the casino and down a couple blocks to this hole in the wall place covered with playbills on the inside walls. We sit in a torn up red vinyl booth and order a pizza.

"So, tell me why you're driving to Vegas for a gig at the Supper Club." Katy starts to pry. "Spill it."

"Well, one of the only things that makes me happy is singing. I was heartbroken and it was my own fault. I learned that it's important to live your life and since I couldn't mend my heart, I put everything I had into my singing. I wasn't getting any traction in LA or Hollywood and decided to start auditioning in different places. Maybe being in the right place at the right time would make a difference. Las Vegas was lucky for me before, so I scheduled six auditions over four days here. I got three positive responses—The Supper Club, a call back to join a lounge band that I didn't hear anything else from after, and then a weird thing that I don't even know what to think about, but I'm counting it positive. I'm not sure, but maybe I belong in Vegas." Trying to be friendly, but giving too much away too quickly.

"So, you really don't have a place to stay when you're here? I don't believe for one second that it's your fault that you were heart broken."

"Believe it. And, no I don't have a place to stay when I'm here. I don't know if I get paid for this gig and my back up plan is to sleep in my truck. I want this to work."

"How was it your fault?" Katy keeps at it.

"Too soon. I don't want to think about it. Give me time to get settled with the newness of the Supper Club stuff and I'll share eventually. I will tell you that stupid things that seem meaningless are sometimes more than they seem." I turn the tables on her. "So, how do you handle the guys?"

"Oh, my babysitting job? Yeah, they know what they want, but don't communicate well and don't know how to make things happen. So, I do it. They're brilliant though and I love them dearly. They know it's all about having the right people around. You'll understand what I mean when the team interacts tomorrow." She stops and gives me a hard look. "You can crash on my couch on your Saturday nights until you figure out what you're doing. Don't stress it."

"Thanks! I really appreciate it. I've been wondering if I could afford a room at the Stardust on Saturday nights, but I'd rather use any extra money to add to my wardrobe and accessories."

"The ladies will take care of you, don't worry about clothes. You'll see. Trust me." Famous last words.

We ate the pizza and continued our casual conversation without any further pressing for details. Then we walked back to the Stardust and parted ways as Katy went back to the Supper Club and I made my way up to room 721.

I unlock the door and walk into my room to find Danny sleeping on my bed. I check the time and it's a few minutes after 11pm. He's stretched out and fully clothed with his work shirt unbuttoned and shoes kicked off onto the floor.

I pull my boots off, slither out of my jeans, and take my top off. Putting everything away where it goes and hanging my top up carefully, in case I need to wear it again. I find Danny's chef coat, pressed and hanging in the closet. I unhook my bra, leaving it sitting on top of the dresser and step out of my panties, dropping them and my socks in the dirty clothes bag. I find my over-worn and partially threadbare Ramones T-shirt that I'd stolen from Danny years ago and pull it on to sleep in. I step into the bathroom quietly, wash my face, and brush out my hair. I turn the radio on low and set an alarm before I climb into my bed with Danny, give him a sweet kiss on the cheek, and snuggle up against him with my head on his shoulder and my arm around his chest. The perfect ending to the day.

At 5am I'm startled when the phone rings and I reach over to answer a wake-up call. I hang up the phone and turn back to Danny gazing at me, melting me with his warm brown eyes. "I love you, Jacks," and he smiles the sweetest smile ever before he pulls me over him and kisses me tenderly. "Babe, I need to check in with the kitchen to find out when the order is getting here this morning." Danny goes to the phone and calls the hotel kitchen, "Hey, what time is the order coming in this morning? I want to get to it first, so I have everything fresh for my Supper Club Menu tonight and time to go buy whatever is missing. Cool. Do you mind if I come down and make myself breakfast before I start work? It'll look like breakfast for two, but you know I eat enough for three people. I really want this chef gig. I know man, thanks. I'll be down in a bit."

Danny comes back to me, kisses me, and rolls me underneath him. He goes to slide his hands up my shirt and finds that I'm pantyless. He slides his hand down to touch my bare skin and notices that I'm wearing his old Ramones T-shirt. "Jacks, you still have this old shirt. Babe, it's got holes in it."

"I don't care. I wear it all the time. It's your shirt and it was all I had." A tear uncontrollably slips from my eye and runs down my face.

"You have me now. I promise, Jacks. You have me now. We'll have each other every weekend and hopefully more, until we can be together everyday, always. I mean it, Jacks." Danny searches my eyes, "It's only you, baby." He kisses me softly, open-mouthed on my lips and then on my throat as he reaches under my shirt with both hands, feeling my breasts, squeezing them gently. He moves one hand to my sex and gets hard against me. He takes his pants off and grabs a condom, before he comes back to me. He runs his hand across my wet heat, curses under his breath and pushes into me slowly, needing me wrapped around him. Slowly burying himself inside me and stretching me little by little. Moans of pleasure slip from his lips as he gets deeper into me. Finally, his base presses against my entrance and his tip finds my magic spot. He sets me on fire with the combination and his deliberate strokes, pushing in all the way and pulling back out. His lips on my neck kissing me and saying the sweetest things I've ever heard, "Someday, Jacks, we'll live together and be together forever. We'll sleep in the same bed together every night. I want to be with you so bad. I want to marry you. I want to give you everything."

Listening to his words, I forget about his touch until I'm screaming out his name and everything has gone dark except the fireworks show exploding in my head. I reach for him, needing to touch him, feel him, grasping for purchase of what-ever piece of him that I can get, "Only you, Danny. Always you," I whisper in his ear. He moves to my lips, sucking on them gently while he continues to move inside me and drive me out of my ever-loving mind. His breathing is ragged and he's rock solid inside me. I arch into him, meeting his strokes. "More baby. Please. I'm yours." The words slip from my lips like a promise. His heart beats hard against mine. He sits up and I watch him examine our connection. I reach down to feel it myself and stroke him lightly with my fingers. He feels amazing, smooth, and stretched to the limit as he starts to pound into me harder and presses on my sensitive nub as if it's a magic button—and it is. He sends me over the edge without notice and goes with me releasing a guttural groan, slamming into me repeatedly while he growls like a tiger. He collapses onto me and holds me tight, sated and in love with me.

I should tell him how strongly I feel for him, but I'm afraid somehow simply saying the words will make everything more difficult, everything will fall apart, or something will happen and he'll be gone. Afraid? You know, I don't often get afraid and last time I let that control me I regretted it. "Danny?"

"Yeah, babe?" He gazes up at me, connecting with my eyes.

"I love you." I smile and warmth fills my heart. Someday it will be us. I've loved him this long and I always will.

Danny kisses me softly and with intent. Our future is in his kiss. He stops abruptly. "Jacks, you know that I come with my daughter?"

"I know that you need your Jackie and your Jacks to make you happy and I want you happy. I wish she was mine."

"You're so perfect. Everyday since she was born, I've wished that she was yours." Danny holds me.

"I need to go to the kitchen and get what I need for the Supper Club Menu. I'll be back and maybe with breakfast."

"I have to be at the Supper Club at 10am for breakfast with the team, but I'm sure your food is better." I remember the tasting from last night. "Danny, the tasting last night was just okay. The chef made French influenced food and it really wasn't what the team likes. He talked about items on his menu that he didn't make for us to try and he didn't have any bread to go with the meal on purpose. Overall, he was kind of pretentious. Katy wants us to ask the chef questions, so don't be surprised if I ask you something about one of your dishes. Be prepared to introduce yourself and your food. Should I not have told you that?"

"I'm glad you did, that helps me know what I want to do."

"Oh, don't skimp on the dessert."

"You can't eat all the desserts."

"Yes I can! The French guy told us about three and only made one—the one I don't like."

Danny gives me a kiss and gets up, putting on his clothes to run down to the kitchen.

"You got this, babe!"

I curl up underneath the blankets and take advantage of the time to get some more sleep, since I already know today is going to be long and I'm going out with Katy tonight.

CHAPTER FIVE

I wake up when the hotel room door opens, and something sweet and savory wafts in to find me making my tummy rumble.

"Good morning, Jacks. I made breakfast to share with you in bed." I look up as he sets a large tray down on the bed and sits down next to me where he belongs. He uncovers a huge platter of French toast and bacon, then pours coffee and adds all the extra stuff to it that makes it good. "Only eat what you want. I know you have breakfast at 10am and I want you to have room for tasting my menu later today. That's why I didn't make too much."

I examine the huge pile of food, "There's enough food there for at least three people!"

Danny smiles and wiggles his eyebrows, "It takes a lot of energy to be me." He leans in and kisses me on the temple, before we completely destroy the plate of food.

"This French toast is to die for! It's the perfect amount of sweet, mmmm tasty!" Danny grins from ear to ear at my compliment.

"Thanks, babe. I need to get to the kitchen and start

working on my dishes for tonight. I have plenty of time, but I want extra time just in case of disaster. I have to go home tonight after work and I'm scheduled to work room service overnight on Saturday."

"I know you need to be with your Jackie. Don't worry about it, Katy says we're going out tonight. I'll see you before I go home Sunday. Remember, I'm coming back next weekend, and the weekend after that, and the weekend after that, and every weekend after that! I'll be here, Danny." I kiss him tenderly, giving him all of my heart. "Go get 'em, chef!"

Danny took off on his mission to be the Supper Club Chef and I could almost smell his piggy mac.

My wake-up call rings as Danny walks out the door and I get up to figure out what I'm wearing today. I need to command attention and respect, not appear to be a kid, and being hot for Danny at the same time would be a plus. I pull on my ripped and holey jeans, then my black suede boots (they really are my favorite) unfolded and wearing them up over my knees. I grab my loose fitting metallic silver, deep v-neck top out of the closet and once again think that I'm missing accessories, a belt at my hips or some jewelry would do wonders. I fluff my hair out, leaving it down long and full. I put on some light make-up, only eyeliner, mascara and lip gloss. I'm ready early, but I make my way to the Supper Club in case they're looking for me, or the fashion police wants to send me back to try again.

I walk into the Supper Club and hear Katy's voice coming from somewhere unknown, "Good morning, hope you slept well. Marni and George would like to see you." Then her tone changes from pleasant and happy to screechy and horrifying, "Where the fuck is my damn coffee?" I hear an exasperated sigh, "Oops. Sorry." And the speaker system clicks off.

I wander back to wardrobe to find George and the other ladies working on various tasks, matching accessories to outfits, sewing, working their way through a closet. Marni is having a conversation with George from across the room. Everything is functioning smoothly, until I walk in.

Marni focuses on me, "I get you first because I only need a minute to test some colors."

George walks up and says, "We can share, I want to show you a couple of costume options."

I watch as they both glare at each other with disgusted expressions, then they turn on me. "What is this that you're wearing, honey?" George asks sweetly.

"Did you start to put make-up on and then forget to finish?" Marni comments out loud and realizes she wasn't internalizing her monologue a few seconds too late. "Your hair looks good."

"I'm not good at this stuff. I go from clothes I can wear in the warehouse, to hard rock outfits to wear on stage in Hollywood, to clothes to wear out dancing—nothing in between except jeans and t-shirts. I hate putting on make-up and my hair is easy. If I'm unacceptable to you, fix me."

Marni and George communicate silently with each other. George smiles happily and claps his hands together like an excited schoolgirl. Marni sits me in her chair and turns me toward the light, "This is going to take a little longer than I said."

Within thirty minutes I've changed clothes three times and I'm now wearing a tunic length red wrap top with a silver chain belt sitting low on my hips and my boobs are taped so I don't give away anything for free. George says the extreme neckline is perfect on me and my bare chest is more dramatic without adding jewelry. Marni nods in agreement with him. The drape of the wrap top makes me feel sexy and eliminates my initial insecurity with the neckline. Marni fluffs my hair out even more and starts my make-up over from scratch, adding a bit of shimmer. It's my reflection in the mirror and I don't even recognize myself, but I love it!

"George, what did you want to show me?"

"Never mind that, I'll take care of your wardrobe for you. You'll have four outfits complete with shoes, jewelry, accessories, etc. all waiting for you here every night you're performing. You can choose which you wear that night and you can change between sets. I'll change out what's on your rack as I see necessary and it won't take long to develop a signature look for you."

"I've got your colors set, so all you have to do is stop and see me after you're dressed and I'll make you stage ready. Bring me sweets or coffee and I'll do your normal every day make-up for you when you're in town."

"You're both amazing! Thank you!" Now I have to trust that they know what they're doing and I think they do.

I want to go find Danny and act like I'm walking a fashion runway for his opinion, but I decide to find Katy for her reaction.

"Look at you! You sexy bitch!" Then under her breath, "… and you're still wearing those jeans. I can't believe George can even make those look good. George truly is a fashion goddess." We both laugh together. "Did you get your make-up and wardrobe handled for dress rehearsal?"

"George and Marni are handling it for me. I'm going with whatever they tell me, they know better than me. Obviously." I gaze down at myself after they got their hands on me.

"Most aren't that trusting, but I think it's the right move. You're going to be the best dressed if you do what they tell you to." Katy focuses on me and her wheels are turning. "The way you're handling this, you're going to steal the show. You know the other singers are either going to hate you or kiss up to you, right?"

"Nah, I'm only going to be here one night a week."

"Jackie, Saturday is the biggest night of the week. They want those set spots."

"Oh shit, well I hope you have my back because you're the queen of everything Supper Club. By the way, have the guys considered a Sunday Brunch Club?" I shouldn't have opened my mouth, but sometimes I have a broken filter.

Katy gives me that look again, you know that 'Hmmm, that's interesting' look. "I don't think so, but I bet it would sell out. Especially considering how many reservations we have already. Also, breakfast has been changed to brunch because the guys are running late, so go play for a bit and be back at 11:30 for brunch."

I take off to wander the Stardust and learn the layout since I'm going to be here quite a bit. I find the food options and shops as I continue to wander. I bump into Tony, who stops in his tracks and stares at me, "Do I know you? Why do you look familiar?"

"Tony, it's Jacks." I turn to him and witness his questioning blank stare. I put on my British accent and try again, "Tony, it's Jacks." I observe his face as his mind is blown.

"Really? I don't remember you being this gorgeous. I mean, always a beaut to behold, but you're beyond that."

"Thank you, I just finished in wardrobe and make-up for the Supper Club. So, I'm professionally styled right now."

"Have you seen Danny?"

"Yea, he made me breakfast this morning."

Tony gestures to his growing size, "He's a great cook. So, he hasn't seen you as you are right now?"

"No, he's busy prepping his tasting menu for the Supper Club today."

"Uh huh, well he needs a break because he needs to see you. Actually, come with me and follow my lead." Tony takes my hand and leads me to the guts of the hotel where the kitchen is. He opens the door slowly, politely leading me through as if he's giving me a tour. "Miss, this is our kitchen and we don't usually bring people through here on a tour like this, but since you asked about our food offerings and preparation I decided we should make an exception. As you can see we have a large kitchen with more than a dozen work stations, cooks, sous chefs, pastry chefs and chefs. Allow me to introduce you to the few that are here now." Tony walks me in a circle around the kitchen until we're standing in front of the two work stations that Danny has commandeered. "This is our top sous chef, Danny." Tony acts like he's introducing him, trying to get his attention.

Without even looking up, "It's very nice to meet you." Then he keeps working. His focus is kind of sexy. At least I know he isn't interested in anybody else.

Tony turns toward me and then back to give Danny the eye, "Look up at what is standing in front of you, jack ass."

Danny stops with an irritated expression on his face that melts immediately as he sees me. "Fuck me, drop dead fucking gorgeous woman of mine."

"That's better." Tony laughs. "You can thank me later. Now I have to get Cinderella back to the Supper Club before she turns into a pumpkin."

"It smells yummy, babe. Sorry to distract you." Then I blow him a kiss and wave as Tony escorts me back to where I belong.

Danny yells out, "Best distraction ever. I need the motivation, Jacks. Rock 'em babe!"

Tony shows me the hotel on our way back to the Supper Club, and finally says what is on his mind, "You're good for him, but it's a challenge for both of you. Stay strong and it'll happen. All of it." Tony walks away to get back to work, but his words ring through me like he's a fortuneteller. I've never considered if I believed in that stuff, but I believe Tony.

CHAPTER SIX

I walk back into the Supper Club in time for Katy to drag me off to brunch. Which, to be fair, was not what you would expect when you're told you're going to have brunch. It was me, Katy, the guys, and whatever food room service decided to send when you called them and requested brunch for four. It wasn't bad, but obviously Danny isn't working room service today. Anyway, the food is not the point, this is more of a meeting than a social gathering.

The guys sit there and stare at Katy until she starts, "Okay, so the guys want you to approve the set lists for all of the other singers. The three of us have discussed your set list and have some instructions for you, so you can finalize your set list as well. Remember that each set is forty-five to fifty minutes long. The guys and I will sit through the individual practices with you, but you will be calling out which songs get run through. I have each of the set lists that the singers submitted and I had the length of each song added for ease of set timing. Feel free to make suggestions, interrupt, or even cut songs off in the middle. We have to get through this. When each singer is done with practice, I'll take over and escort them to wardrobe and make-up. If something stands out to you about their style, George finds that helpful to know. Do you have any questions?"

"Can I suggest songs that aren't on their set list?"

"Yes."

"Do I have to care if they don't know the song and need to learn it?"

"No."

"I'm going to need a notebook, a pen and a couple high-lighters. Can I get two copies of each set list? When do you want the final set lists?"

"We should be done with run-throughs by 3pm tomorrow. Most of them are today. By 5pm on Saturday would be great and I'll make sure the stuff you need is waiting for you when we start run-throughs."

"Is the band here for run-throughs?"

"Yes, and they have each set list already."

"I appreciate the trust you're putting in me. What's the bald guy's name that leads the band?"

"Archie."

"Okay, I'm going to talk with him before we start. How long do we have until we start?"

"First singer is already here and scheduled to start in twenty minutes."

"I'm going to leave you three to whatever it is you do, okay?"

"Yes, go ahead." Kyle finally says something, James is still silent.

I go back stage to find Archie and go over communication. We talk about what we want from the singers and I let him know that I'm open to any suggestions.

"Alright, ladies and gentlemen, let's do this!" Katy gets things moving.

I join them at the table and the first singer walks out on

stage. I review her set list and quickly pick a song that should be good for the Supper Club. I listen while I peruse the set list she submitted and I'm having a hard time imagining some of these songs at the Supper Club. After the first song, "Do you have a special arrangement of 'Free Bird,' 'I'm Too Sexy,' or 'Push It' that you want to use at the Supper Club?"

"No, those are my jams," she changes her stance and gives me a little attitude.

"Archie, any ideas for making those have the Supper Club sound?"

"Not really, I'm sure we can figure something out if we need to." Archie keeps his laugh to himself.

We get through all the songs on the set list that could work for the Supper Club and she has extra time in the set.

"Archie, let's try 'I'm Too Sexy.' Can we maybe slow it down a bit and add a slight swing to the chorus?" I get a nod from Archie and a horrified wide-eyed stare from the singer, but we all make it through it.

I turn to Katy, "Can I have her come back at the end of run-throughs tomorrow and anybody else that might have issues like this?"

"Sure. You can have her come back later today or in an hour, whatever you think is best. We want the music to be right."

I confirm with Katy and the guys, "I need a few minutes to review the other set lists, and I'd like to join her on stage with a couple of song suggestions."

There's silent communication between the three of them, "Give it a shot," Katy smiles and nods.

I address the singer, "Bear with me a few minutes please." I glance at Archie and he throws me a shaka.

I stand up to join the first singer on stage and Katy pulls me over to whisper in my ear, "Don't strangle her while you're up there. In fact, don't touch her at all, we don't need the lawsuit." She was only halfway kidding. It makes me laugh as I walk up the steps to the stage.

I offer my hand to shake with the singer, "I'm Jackie. It's nice to meet you. My goal is to make your set more Supper Club style and help you be the best you can be."

She gives me a hard 'who the fuck are you?' stare.

"Do you know 'Baby, I Love Your Way' or 'Walk on the Wild Side?'" I wait for a response from her, but all I get is a blank stare. "No problem."

"Archie, you guys know 'Walk on the Wild Side,' right?"

"Of course." Archie gets a big grin and the guys in the band begin fidgeting around.

"I think it would be a great addition for the Supper Club. Can you 60's it up for me? I want to sing it for her and find out what the guns think." I love Archie. He has the band playing around and ready to go before I can shut my mouth. The band plays it exactly how I want it. I sing the first verse and the chorus, then signal to stop and wait for approval. I get thumbs up all around, except from the singer I'm on stage with.

"I don't know that song," she glares at me with extreme irritation.

"You can learn it and you will sound great singing it," I smile at her. "Arch, can the band play 'Baby I Love Your Way'? The Freebird version? Leaning toward the Will To Power remake."

Archie gives me an, 'I see what you did there' gaze of affirmation and the music starts. I sing the first couple of lines, all of the sudden she knows this song and I pass the mic to her. I signal for the band to play the whole thing including the Freebird part and make my way back to the trio sitting at the table.

The singer finishes the song and is happy with the Freebird part. "I want you to learn 'Walk on the Wild Side' and come back to sing it for us before the end of the day." She gives me a blank stare.

Katy pipes in, "Come back about 7pm. Thank you."

I turn to the trio, "Is that what you wanted me to do?"

James speaks, "It's more than we expected."

"You need to pick up the pace, or we're going to run out of time," Katy always a taskmaster.

"Reschedule one of them to after the dinner break. Quick doesn't always get the best results." Did Kyle say two complete sentences? "Katy, Jackie doesn't need us for this. Hang with her so she has some back up and take some notes for us, please." The guys get up and go wherever it is they go to do whatever it is they do.

Fuck yeah! Better than I ever imagined. All I wanted was the opportunity to sing and be heard. Hope to be able to one day make a living with my singing. And here I am, not only singing two sets every Saturday night, but choosing what music will be performed every night, every set, by every vocalist.

"Katy, can we take five in between? I need to step outside a minute and grab a soda. I'm sure the band would like to stretch their legs." I smile and wait for her response.

"Let's do that. Take five guys. Singer #2, please be on stage in five. Thank you." Katy continues to handle business.

I take a quick walk through the casino and try to remember where the sundry shop is, so I can grab a can of Dr. Pepper.

Tony catches me wandering again, "What are you doing now?"

"Where's the store? I need soda and maybe a snack. I've got less than five minutes." I look at him like 'save me please!' I wonder what Tony does? Professional at rescuing damsels in distress maybe?

Tony leads me to the store and I grab my addictions, Dr. Pepper, Peanut M&M's and a snack size bag of potato chips.

The girl behind the counter rings me up and Tony tells her, "Give her the employee discount. She's new here," and flashes his ID Card, magically dropping the price in half. "I'm here until 8pm tonight. If you need anything, simply pick up a house phone and ask the operator to transfer you to walkie 4."

"Thank you, Tony," and I take off back to the Supper Club quickly with snacks in hand.

I sit down at the table with Katy, pop open my soda and drop my snacks on the table, offering to share. We get going with singer #2 and make our way through all of the vocalists that are doing their run-through today. Some better than others, but all of them needing some adjustment. About halfway through I realize that I still need to cut down my own set list and there may be some songs that would work for one of the other singers. I read the notes from the guys on my set list and take a few minutes with Archie to make the hardest set decisions, mine. I cross things off my set list and give it to Katy in its final form:

1. "Get Here" by Oleta Adams
2. "I Can't Make You Love Me" by Bonnie Raitt
3. "Stay" by Lisa Loeb
4. Beatles Medley (Here Comes the Sun/Blackbird/Golden Slumbers/Dear Prudence/Two Of Us/I Will/If I Fell/And I Love Her/In My Life)
5. "Black Velvet" by Alannah Myles
6. "What About Me" by Moving Pictures
7. "Come To My Window" by Melissa Etheridge
8. "What I Am" by Edie Brickell and the New Bohemians
9. "Beautiful In My Eyes" by Joshua Kadison
10. "Show Me the Way" by Styx
11. "To Be With You" by Mr. Big

I make it through the vocalists scheduled before the dinner break and we have some time until the tasting is scheduled. I love most music and the Supper Club is a lot of fun, but I need to let my rock and roll heart loose. Before Katy leaves me, "Does anybody around here have any objections to rock a bit on the harder side?"

"No..." she stares at me like where am I going with this.

"Great, do you need me for anything before the tasting?"

"I don't think so." Katy isn't sure what to do and that doesn't happen often. I get up and beeline for Archie.

"Hey, we have a little time before dinner. You guys want to light this place up with something a little harder?" I wait for a response. I'm sure they can all see the anticipation and excitement in my eyes.

Archie turns to the band and gets nods all around. "I think we need it."

"Me, too." I grin, hardly able to contain myself.

Archie starts, "We heard you rocked some Aerosmith at your audition. Let's try it live." He counts them down and they hit the music hard. The melody flows through me and my body relaxes into my zone as I start to sing "Crazy" without holding back my rock instincts.

The crew comes popping out of everywhere to find out who's on stage, and by the end of the song I have a crowd gathered in front of me like a rock star. I turn to the band and give them props, they did an awesome job. Archie gives me an acknowledging nod, "We have time for a couple more before break. Are you up for a challenge?"

"Bring it!" I glare at the band and wait for them to play. The music starts, the slow bass beat and groove of Journey's "Lovin' Touchin' Squeezin'" takes my body over. I can't help but move to the groove. I turn to the band and give them an approving catcall. Mic in hand I wander the stage giving each of the guys in the band attention as I sing, until I get to the chorus and move back to the mic stand, letting go with Steve Perry style.

The crowd has grown while I wasn't paying attention, the guys are here as well as casino security and some of the workers from around the hotel. Tony is with security, wait—Tony is security. The volume did get turned up, maybe we're in trouble for being too loud and disturbing the casino? The volume hasn't been disconnected, so that must not be the problem. The song comes to an end and I'm beaming at the response I get from the crowd, including the whole security crew in the back that's chanting 'Jackie.' The guys without guns are smiling from ear to ear and keep looking at each other. I search for Katy, "Katy! Do we have time for one more before the tasting?"

Katy pops up in the crowd from behind the guys, "Yes and the guys would like to hear you do Janis."

I nod and turn to Archie, "Janis? 'Piece of My Heart?' You guys got that one, right?" Archie steps up front with me on guitar for the intro and works the crowd. I start to rub my hands across my face and remember I'm in full make-up, so I stretch my arms up crossing my wrists and bring them down to my sides slowly, closing my eyes as I start to sing. I open my eyes to find I've got Archie's respect. Then I survey the room to find James and Kyle singing along, and Tony staring at me in disbelief. Encouragement takes me by surprise and I sing the last verse without holding anything back. It feels fantastic! The song ends and the room erupts, like nothing I've ever experienced before—this is where I belong. I tell the band they're great and move off the stage because it's time for the tasting and the last thing I want to do is make Danny wait.

CHAPTER SEVEN

K aty shouts out to the crew, "Tasting time ladies and gentlemen! Please get to the table quickly. We have more work to do tonight. That was some great pre-dinner entertainment from Jackie and the Archies." She ends with applause and turns to the guys to read the situation.

I join the trio at the table, sitting in the same place I did for the tasting last night. I stop and consider the tasting with Danny. I'm confident the food is going to be delish and everybody is going to absolutely love it. Will they be able to tell there's something between Danny and I? I don't want that to be a problem or impact their chef choice.

Katy stands up, "Okay, ladies and gentlemen, this is tasting #2. This is a completely separate chef and menu option. You should be comparing the two and thinking about which one you like better. Now, this is Sous Chef Danny and this would be his first Chef position."

"Hey everybody, I'm Danny and I can't wait for you to try my food. The Supper Club should be a place that makes people happy and nothing does that better than good music and comfort food. I was asked to provide small portions, so you could try more things. Please keep in mind that these are menu options and not necessarily things you would order together in one meal. I hope you enjoy my food. To start I'm offering a green salad with fresh herbs dressed in balsamic vinaigrette, Caprese Salad with a Bite, Roasted Beets with Goat Cheese and Toasted Walnuts, Creamed Tomato Soup accented with Parm Rind and Chicken Noodle Soup." Simply having him in the room sends my body into high alert. Danny looks at me and I smile, but try not to draw any attention. "For my entrees I'm offering Spaghetti with Meatballs, Penne Alfredo, Bacon Cheeseburger Sliders with Steak Fries and Bacon Ketchup, Citrus Marinated Chicken with Seasonal Vegetables, and my Piggy Mac. All served with choice of Garlic Toast or Soft Rolls." I need to get a gym membership or I'm going to be fat. Katy and the guys are drooling. "Lastly, dessert is dear to my heart and I'm offering a Traditional Hot Fudge Sundae, Apple Pie a la Mode, and Brownies to Make Blondie Love You with Lightly Sweetened Fresh Whipped Cream. I know there is a lot of food and I hope you enjoy it. Does anybody have any questions about anything?" Danny smiles, thinking he's being smart and offering to answer questions before Katy does it.

Katy starts, "Thank you, Danny. What is Piggy Mac?"

"My young daughter named it. It's Macaroni and Cheese made with a mixture of Cheddar and Italian Cheeses, that has bacon and my slow roasted pulled pork mixed into it. It's her favorite thing to eat."

"It's delicious." Katy's plate is clean.

"I have more if you would like it."

"I'll remember that. Also, what is Brownies to Make Blondie Love You?" Katy focuses on him curiously. "I get that they're brownies, but what makes them enough to make someone love you?"

"I created the recipe for one specific person knowing they have a sweet tooth and what flavors they like the most. This is a chocolate fudge brownie layered with a peanut butter blondie. The name is a play on the words brownie and blondie."

"And, let me guess—she's a blonde?"

"Yes, she is and the first time she ate this dessert," Oh no... don't say it, don't say I made orgasm noises! "well I knew she loved it."

"Thank you, Danny. Does anybody else have any questions?" Katy looks around to find that everybody is too busy eating to even acknowledge her. She looks at me, wanting a question asked.

"Um, are you concerned about serving bread, that it might fill your diners up so they aren't able to eat your food?"

"Not at all. I want the customer to be happy and if that means they need to get that last bit of sauce off the plate with a roll or can't enjoy a meal without garlic toast—either way they need to get what they want. I think my food speaks for itself and the diner can decide what they want to eat."

"What meal would you suggest to diners ordering from your menu?"

"I think everything is great, but I would suggest Green Salad with Herbs, the Piggy Mac with Garlic Toast, and the Brownie to Make Blondie Love You. It's balanced and tasty, with the perfect ending."

Katy chimes in, "Thank you. Everything is wonderful. You're dismissed, Danny." Danny leaves the room. Katy turns to the guys and finds them still buried in their plates of food. "You two like this menu or are you just hungry?" They both glance up at her and go immediately back to eating. "Please enjoy the food and I can see most of you are or already have. Take a minute to complete the survey card regarding each dish and make a comment about the food or chef overall. Thank you!" She turns to me, then back to the room, "Show of hands, who likes this menu better than the menu Chef Francois presented last night?" Everyone in the room raises their hand. "We have one more tasting tomorrow night."

Katy and I sit together finishing our meal and chatting casually, while we wait for everyone to finish and give her their survey cards. I finally get to my brownie and it's still warm. I get some of the brownie and some of the whipped cream together on my fork, and put it in my mouth.

Katy looks at me funny, "What was that?"

"What?"

"Really? You shivered and made a yummy noise."

"Oh. I like dessert." Crap.

Katy looks at the top of my head and nods without saying another word. Then a few minutes later, "So, do you know Danny?"

"Yes. I hadn't seen him in years and then he was here serving food when I was auditioning." No way to hide it without lying and besides, it happened when I auditioned.

"So, how well do you know Danny?" Katy starts questioning.

"Katy, do you know Danny or his friends or co-workers? How long have you known him?" I'm concerned that I'll say the wrong thing. I'm a secret.

Katy glares at me strangely, "I know he's been working room service and that I've seen him around the hotel since I started working here on this project a couple months ago. He seems nice. He's very nice to look at and he's an amazing cook. That's all. Oh, and whoever the blonde is—she's lucky."

I smile at Katy, "I'd prefer not to talk about this here and I either need a gym membership or more nights on stage." She winks at me and lets it go.

We move on to the last run-through for the day and then meet with the handful of returning vocalists that needed to work on songs, learn songs, whatever. Nothing too horrible or great for that matter.

CHAPTER EIGHT

It's almost 8pm, so I find a house phone and ask for walkie 4. Tony comes on the line "This is Tony," sounding all business.

"Hey Tony, this is Jackie. I saw you in the room earlier and just wanted to thank you for your support."

"Thank me? Honey, you must be kidding. You don't need my support, you've got this in spades. I'm still trying to figure out how Danny got so lucky. Honestly, you have an amazing talent and you'll be here more nights, maybe in more places. This is where you belong and what you should be doing. Great job. I didn't know you did this, surprised me."

"I still appreciate it! Can I ask, do you know if Danny's still here or gone for the night?"

"He's gone home to his little Jackie. If mama bitch is home tonight, he might be back later."

"Thanks for the info. I'm going out with Katy tonight, so it's good timing. He needs to spend time with Jackie. I need to get to know Katy, she's going to let me crash on her couch when I'm here on Saturday nights."

"Good, she's good people and part of the production crew. She doesn't know people from the Stardust."

"Are you saying she can know about me and Danny? Because that would make my life easier."

"That's your call, Ms. Secret. Can you trust her?"

"Yes and she's too sharp, she'll figure it out. She may have already just seeing the two of us in the room together."

"Good luck, girl. Be careful out there." Tony hung up.

I find Katy, "What's the plan tonight? Where are we going? What are we doing? Do I need to go change?"

Katy laughs, "You're non-stop! All day and still ready to go out."

"Duh! Yeah! Let's go!"

"You don't need to change, but I do. How do you feel about lounge hopping the strip and dancing?"

"That's perfect. Just us or who else is going?"

"Probably just us, but sometimes I get tagalongs. I need a few minutes. Why don't you go find Marni and George and see if they want to re-style you for night time?"

"Okay. You know where to find me." I head off to wardrobe and make-up.

"Hey Marni, I'm going out to play on the strip tonight. Should I change my make-up or anything?"

Before Marni can answer, I hear George from across the room, "Yes, and I have an outfit I want you to try."

Marni shakes her head at me, "Do his part first."

George holds up this flashy outfit that is beyond, beyond, beyond anything that I would ever wear. I stare at him in fear, ready to say no way and he hangs it up pulling out another outfit instead. Thank goodness. Still not quite me, but not the other thing. Wait. I think George may have used psychology against me. Whatever. I'll look great. "George, is this costuming for the show or clothes to wear out tonight?"

"Clothes to wear out tonight."

"I'm not comfortable going out without a date in a skirt that short." I tell him the truth and I don't want to get hit on. I have Danny.

"That's what hot pants are for," and he shoves some in my face. "Besides, you won't feel like your skirt is that short with your over the knee boots on."

I change into the short spandex mini skirt with hot pants on underneath and pull my boots back on. When I go back to change the top, George stops me and says, "I actually like it with the red top, you should stay like that. Now, go see Marni and I'll get you a metal choker and some bangles."

"Yes, ma'am!"

"Get moving, gorgeous. Marni is waiting for you." George swats me away.

I walk up to Marni and she gestures for me to sit in her chair. She turns me around into the light and cleans up my make-up, adding darker eyeliner and some shiny glitz to high-light my features and my bare chest. Then she moves on to my hair, simply brushing it out and fluffing it.

George walks over and adds accessories, "We really should start taking photos of you when we have you styled. Katy and the guys are going to need photos for the advertising and signage. We could use them for our package, too." Marni nods in agreement and pulls out her camera. With no warning I'm being posed with lighting. My life. There is no way this is my life.

I find Katy again and she's already changed to go out. "Are you ready to go?"

"I was, but not now that I've seen you. George! Help me, please." She calls out and George is there instantly. "I'm going out with Jackie tonight. Fix me please."

"We didn't know. We would've toned it down a bit. Come with me," and we follow George back to wardrobe. "Marni, Katy is going to need you in a few minutes," George calls out across the room as he steps into a walk-in closet and shuffles around. He comes back out with a black pleather skirt that's not short enough to require hot pants, red fuck me pumps and a sheer black top for Katy to wear over the strappy camisole she has on.

Marni takes over and does her make-up, then brushes out her long straight red hair with some chemical that somehow makes it straighter and shiny.

"We should've photographed them together. Look at them. They're hot." George goes on and on to Marni, and the guys hear them as they're walking by.

Kyle sticks his head around the corner, "Who is the 'they' that are hot?" Then he focuses on us. "Shit, they're hot. Where are you ladies going?"

"Out." Katy answers quickly and abruptly.

"You have dates tonight or are you going out like that alone?" Kyle asks not liking Katy's answer.

"We aren't going alone. We have each other." Katy is in smart-ass mode.

"Uh huh. James, look at these ladies." James peeks over Kyle's head and gives Kyle a nudge. "Okay then, so where are we going? James and I will be your escorts for the night."

My turn, "We don't need escorts. We'll be fine. Big girls and all."

Katy turns to me rolling her eyes, "Give it up. Once they decide, you can't change it. But, they'll have to keep up and at least they don't make much noise." We both giggle. "Let's go!"

The night was crazy. We took off on foot and Katy knew all the lounges with good music. She knew the musicians and took time to introduce me. Even talked me up and got me on stage to sing a few times. She may have been charging a finders fee, not sure and I don't care. The guys followed us around like lost puppy dogs. Lounges and dance clubs are totally not their scene, which is kind of funny considering they're opening the Supper Club and obviously have an appreciation for music. Eyes were on us everywhere we went. I admit we were hot, both professionally styled wearing black and red. I caught Kyle checking out Katy, and James is there because, well I don't know why.

By the end of the night, we're all slightly more than buzzed. Kyle has been putting his arm around Katy and there's something interesting going on there. James is flirting with the cocktail waitresses and seems to know every single one of them by name, odd for a guy that rarely speaks—though he's good looking with that slender body, so maybe they don't care if he talks.

I'm happy to be out and enjoying the music. I don't want anyone hitting on me or touching me. I only want Danny and I don't want any weirdness with one of the guys or any of the crew members. I'm getting attention from men around me and a couple have asked me to dance, but I've been able to brush them off and dance with Katy. It's getting late and I start to wonder if Danny stayed home or got out of the house because mama bitch, as Tony so eloquently put it, was home. I find a pay phone and call the Stardust to check my messages. The operator rings my message through to me: "Hey Jacks, I'm home with Jackie tonight. She's not home tonight. I hope you're having fun and I wish I was out with you. Be safe and I'll find you at the Supper Club tomorrow tonight. I still have your extra room key. I wish you could be here with us. Bye babe." Simply hearing his words make my heart warm.

"Katy, what time are we starting in the morning?"

"You should be there about 10am. No need for a breakfast meeting to discuss being hung over and too tired."

"Alright, then I'm going to head back since it's getting late and the guys are taking care of you."

"Are you wussing out on me?"

"You look like you have some business to handle with Kyle and James has some business with a handful of cocktail girls. It's been a long day and I still need to review set lists."

Katy stares at me like there should be more, "And…?"

"And, I might be expecting a phone call."

"From…?"

"Can't talk about that here. We will talk about it soon and when it's only you and me."

"Why are you so mysterious?" Katy's intrigued.

"I don't mean to be. I appreciate everything you do and you letting me crash at your place next Saturday. This has all been crazy for me. I need to figure out how to do everything and still get things done, you know like laundry and grocery shopping. Shit. I didn't even tell Bryan I was leaving early, I'll have to smooth that over when I get back and he'll probably be waiting on my doorstep." Sometimes I rattle on when I should shut up.

"Bryan? How many men do you have?"

"Oh, only one. Bryan is a musician friend. It's complicated." I want to change this line of questioning and go for the pivot, "I can't believe we open next weekend. I'm so excited!"

"Nice try Goldilocks. Or should I call you Blondie?"

"Very clever Little Red Riding Hood, but I'm not discussing it in public and I'm not discussing it around the guys." Firm statement and I hope she gets the point. "Now what's up with you and Kyle? He's into you."

"Yea, he wants me. He doesn't like me to go out without being there to protect me. He's the boss and I know he's not a traditional boss, but he's still the boss. We have known each other since we were teenagers. The three of us had classes together in high school. They needed help then, too."

"So, are you into Kyle or James or what?"

"Truth? We had a threesome in high school and it was so awkward. Nothing since."

No fucking way. "Are you serious?"

"No, I'm kidding." Katy laughs and now I don't know if she was joking or not. "I'm getting punchy. We should go back to the Stardust."

We all hop in a cab and go back to the Stardust. I get the set lists from the Supper Club to take back to my room and Katy goes in to take care of something at her desk with Kyle right behind her. James disappears somewhere on the way in.

CHAPTER NINE

I get to my room and find a note on my pillow:

Jacks,
There's a box with brownies on the dresser and
whipped cream in the mini fridge. I wore this shirt
today and wanted to leave you one that didn't have
holes.
Love,
Danny

The T-shirt smells like him and it's a Skid Row concert shirt. I check the dresser and sure enough a box sits there waiting for me. I open the box to find six of the fudgy blondie brownies. I immediately go to the phone and call down to the Supper Club. "This is Katy. What fool is calling me here at this hour?"

"Hey Katy, stop working and come up to my room. You can crash here if you want tonight. I have dessert and enough to share."

"Is there chocolate involved?"

"Yes."

"I'll be up in ten minutes. Room 721, right?"

"Yep. Don't take too long. I can't promise I won't eat it all," and I hang up.

I wash my face, tie my hair up in a knot, and change into sweatpants and Danny's Skid Row T-shirt. Then my phone rings, "Hello?"

"Hey baby. I just want to make sure you're in safe for the night and found my note."

"Yes, you're so sweet. Thank you. I just changed into your Skid Row T-shirt and I'm ready to eat your yummy brownies."

"Did you have fun tonight?"

"Yes, but I would rather have been with you." I say sweetly. "How's Jackie?"

"She's asleep right now. My sweet angel fell asleep in front of the TV again, so I built a blanket fort around her." This man kills me with his sweetness and love for his girl.

"Katy is coming up to have a brownie with me. Um, I need to tell her about you and me. She already suspects and I'm going to be staying at her place on Saturdays. Are you okay with that? I think she's safe."

"I trust your judgment, Jacks. She definitely doesn't hang in the same groups as Jackie's mom, and she's sharp, so she'll catch on. Better to tell her."

"Good. I wanted to tell you that everybody loved your food at the tasting tonight. So much better than the first tasting. Almost all of the plates were clean when we were done."

"Tony told me he watched you perform this afternoon and that you were unbelievable."

"We had a little time before the dinner break, so the band and I let it rock. Needed to break up the Supper Club style a little. It was great. They're having me finalize the set lists for all the vocalists. I can't even put into words how amazing that is."

"Jacks, that's freaking awesome!" There was silence, "Babe, am I going to be in your way? I don't want to hold you back."

Stunned, "Danny, none of it's worth it if I can't share it with you. It's me and you, Danny. Whatever it takes."

The warmth of his smile in his voice, "You really are perfect. Go eat my brownies and I'll see you later tonight, baby. I miss you," and he hangs up in time for the knock on my door. I check the peephole and let in Katy.

"Come on in. I have extra clothes if you want to change."

"I've got it covered, I keep clothes in my desk." She shows me the bag in her hand and steps into the bathroom to change. She comes back out and says, "So, where's the chocolate?"

I open the box of brownies, get the whipped cream out, and find that Danny left napkins and forks for me. I hand one over to Katy and she digs in. "These are the Brownies to Make Blondie Love You." Katy states very clearly.

"Yep. Hi, I'm blondie. But, including you there are only four of us that know that and it's a secret. It needs to stay a secret. Are you okay with that?" I turn to Katy for confirmation.

"Whatever you say. But, why are you a secret?" I hoped she wouldn't ask, but knew she would.

"A few years ago we were casually dating and it wasn't going anywhere because it was all based on a lie. He accidentally knocked up his co-worker and since he always does the right thing he moved in with her with plans to marry her, but he couldn't marry her because he doesn't love her and she holds that against him. They aren't together or anything, they just live in the same apartment with their daughter. She knows what I look like, but not what my name is and she thinks I've been out of the picture for years—and I had been until I auditioned for the Supper Club. She thinks I'm the reason that he won't be with her and she's jealous of a picture of me and him together. When we saw each other at my audition it was like we'd never been apart and I was happy for the first time in years. He told me to go on with my life and forget him because I deserve better, that I shouldn't have to be a secret. But, for him I'm happy and willing to be a secret if that protects his daughter. He's a great dad and he's afraid of the mom taking his daughter away from him. She knows he's dating again, but not that it's me and we don't go out in public together. Okay?"

"Tell me about the lie." Katy stares at me sternly, but happily eating brownies.

"I hate this part. Here it goes. When I met Danny I was in Vegas for the weekend with a friend of mine and we were using British accents as part of a homework assignment for our choir group. We were in Vegas for a weekend having fun and playing around. I spent almost eight hours with Danny that night as a British chick and we had even made up a backstory to go with it. At the end of the night, we were very heated and the attraction was crazy. We talked on the phone over the next few days and he said he called because he wanted to hear my voice, which was still the British accent. Then I came to Vegas for a weekend and stayed with him, still using the accent and I'm not proud of this, but I didn't tell him the truth because I was afraid it would end it and I didn't want it to end—for over six months. Then my friend that was with me when it started caught on that I hadn't told him and came to Vegas with me and made me tell him, but he told me about knocking up his co-worker before I could tell him about the accent and it was pretty much over. So, I told him about the accent and he didn't hold it against me, in fact he likes California Girls better than British. It was a horrible realization and my fault that I hadn't told him sooner and allowed the relationship to progress. We weren't exclusive, but we would have been if I hadn't lied. Anyway, the only things that matter are that it's a secret and needs to stay that way, and we love each other. End of story."

"And don't forget that he's an outstanding cook, my fudgy goodness these are good." Katy talking with her mouth full.

"He really is the sweetest, and the reason I need to get a gym membership or find more high energy gigs."

"I get it and I've got your back on this. No worries, Jackie."

"Thank you. I know it's stupid, but I also know I won't always be a secret. There's a someday out there with our name on it. He named his daughter Jackie and he calls me Jacks. She's a beautiful little blonde girl and looks just like him, not at all like her brunette mother."

"Wow. Don't worry, I won't tell anyone."

I smile and hand Katy more whipped cream. We eat ourselves into a sugar coma and pass out.

CHAPTER TEN

A few minutes before 7am I'm woken up by a digital alarm that I've never heard before, that's immediately followed by Katy yelling out, "Fuck! It can't be 7am already."

"It's Saturday. Go back to sleep and go in a little later. There's no way the guys are there this early." I sound groggy and don't open my eyes.

"It's Saturday." I hear some beeps, Katy rolls over and goes back to sleep.

8:45am repeat of the digital alarm, "I have to be at the club with the door unlocked by 9am." Katy is up, in the shower, dressed and out the door in under fifteen minutes. Impressive.

My wake up call rings at 9am, but I pull the blankets up over my head and pretend I'm in a fort with Danny. I can smell him on his shirt and when I close my eyes, I imagine his touch as if he's here with me.

I sit up quickly and grab the set lists from the nightstand when I realize that I didn't work on finalizing the set lists yet. As I read through the lists, I'm happy to find that my notes will be enough to finish everything up. I don't want to cut some songs until I've listened to all of the run-throughs. There are some song duplications and I want the singer that performs it best to get the song on their set list.

I get ready quickly. Washing up, pulling on my faded black jeans, suede boots, and thumbing through the closet for a top to wear—but, I don't know why because George will probably make me change anyway. I put on a snug fitting purple stretchy tank top and my black suede vest. I brush out my hair and go without make-up, comfortable in my own skin.

I make my way to the Supper Club early, hoping Katy has coffee. I walk in to find everyone working away and a pot of coffee waiting for me to pour a cup. I find Katy and check in with her, "Good morning. Do I have an assignment this morning or do I have time to work on set lists and visit with George and Marni?"

"First run-through is scheduled for 11am." She glances up at me, "No make-up? Please go find Marni," she looks me up and down, "and George." I give her a salute and wander over to wardrobe.

"Good morning, Marni. Please tell me where to find the best donuts, so I can bring some with me tomorrow." I walk up to Marni with my bare face and smile.

"Do I hear Jackie?" George calls out from somewhere hidden and comes walking out with his arms full of clothes. He examines me and I wait to hear what the problem with my outfit is today.

"Remember, I'm not good at this and I'm willing to be fixed." I put my kind smile in place.

"You always wear those boots. The faded black jeans aren't bad. I like the vest, but it kind of hides your figure. Not sure about the plain purple tank top. The outfit suits you. I'll get you some accessories and let you pass for today, but only because I want you to have an open mind for costume and remember tomorrow is dress rehearsal." George has an anxiously evil expression on his face. He's been waiting for tomorrow.

I sit in Marni's chair, "I can't believe you showed up here with no make-up. Crazy girl," as she applies my make-up for me, flawlessly. Then she takes a few minutes and gives my hair big curls. George gives me a belt with a simple, rhinestone buckle and has me tuck in my tank top. He puts a silver disheveled hoop necklace around my neck with an amethyst amulet hanging from it and turns to Marni. "I'm thinking of pulling it back on one side."

"Perfect," apparently George and Marni communicate like everybody else around here, but as long as George agrees it's probably good. Marni pulls my hair back on one side, tucking it behind my ear and George switches my small studs out for matching silver disheveled hoop earrings. "It really is amazing what we can do in just a few minutes."

"It is. Thank you both so much." I speak genuinely and bow in thanks.

I sit at the table with the set lists, comparing the run-throughs scheduled for today with those that we already heard, and Archie sits beside me, looking over my shoulder at my notes. "Good morning, do you have any feedback on the sets we heard yesterday?"

Archie takes my notes from yesterday and reviews them carefully. "Actually, I agree with your notes. But, the band doesn't like to play a couple of the songs and I thought maybe you could cut those." He draws an X next to the songs he would like to go away and I'm not in love with either one of them, so I cross them off the list. Archie gives me a high five and moves onto the stage.

I finalize the set lists that don't have any overlap with today's run-throughs and have the others ready to go with a few pen strokes. I find Katy to give her the set lists that are finalized and she's not alone, in fact Kyle is wrapped around her. "Umm, leaving these on your desk and going to find sugar. I'll bring you some, too," and I take off quickly for the casino. I walk up to the coffee shop where there's a pastry case with muffins and donuts and all kinds of sweets. I buy a variety of donuts and muffins, and take them back to share at the club. I walk back to Katy's office and set a chocolate donut on her desk while I have my eyes covered.

"Seriously?" Katy berates me. "What did you think you would see?"

"I have no idea, and it doesn't matter as long as you like it. Enjoy your donut." I get out of there before I'm tempted to ask about Kyle and inhale my second donut as I walk over to the table and wait for run-throughs to start.

Overall the vocalists on Saturday were better than those on Friday. The few times I questioned a song being appropriate for the Supper Club, the singers actually had an arrangement in mind or agreed that it might not be right for the venue. The set lists were easy to finish up. I delivered the finalized set lists to Katy and she stared at me in surprise, "That's it? Already done? You aren't putting me off until tomorrow? And, you completed run-throughs on schedule?"

"Yes. Don't look so surprised. I hope the set lists are what the guys are looking for."

"Oh, the guys want you to add a Janis song to your set list."

"No problem. Does that mean I need to cut something else or it's okay for me to go over a few minutes?"

"Yes. Whichever you want. Also, plan on some practice time with the vocalists tomorrow after the dress rehearsal. You will want to give each of them some things to work on. Trust me on that. Now, go provide pre-dinner entertainment for the crew."

No argument from me. I walk out on stage and Archie

starts, "Ready to jam before dinner break? The band has some songs in mind for you."

"Hell yeah!" I give him a big grin and hear the keyboard intro to Bon Jovi's "Runaway." I know it's an opportunity to wail. The crew hoots and hollers from all over the venue as they start to shuffle out to watch. The band starts the next song without even taking a breath and I'm thrilled to hear "Edge of a Broken Heart" by Vixen because I know it better than most songs. It's always been one of those songs that stuck with me. The hard rock bands I played with in Hollywood wanted me to sing it. I absorb the applause and it builds my confidence.

Katy yells out, "Only time for two more."

"Up for something moody?" Archie asks before they start the next song.

"I'm singing whatever you throw at me," and I give him a nod.

The next thing I hear is the drums thrumming out the beginning of Jefferson Airplane's "White Rabbit." I focus on Grace Slick in my mind and her drawn out vocals that grow with intensity as the song progresses. It's exhilarating. I lose myself in the song and find I'm standing at the mic with my eyes closed, belting at the top of my lungs at the end of the song. I get applause from the band and nothing means more.

"Changing it up again, since we finally got the piano here," Archie says. I didn't know we had a piano for the Supper Club. It adds a new dynamic and possibilities for song arrangements. I'm driven to sit at the piano and play for myself, but that's not my place here. Then I hear the solo piano introduction to "Let It Be" by the Beatles and it's a no brainer, great song. I sing without even thinking since Beatles music has been in my life since conception and I love everything they did. But, I can't help but think about the piano greats and the music they've written. By the end of the song I've got the whole crew singing along and we're having fun. The room is happy and clapping.

"It's that time again, ladies and gentlemen. Please join us for the third and last tasting. Great work getting us all warmed up." Katy nods to the stage and claps.

I join Katy and the guys for the third night in a row, thinking that maybe the guys will loosen up a bit—but they don't change.

"This is tasting #3, ladies and gentlemen. Again, this menu is completely separate from the other two you have experienced. Please compare it to the others and use your survey cards for each dish. Tonight we decide who our chef will be." Katy takes a breath and continues, "Please welcome Chef Clarke."

"Hello all, I'm Chef Clarke. When I think Supper Club, I think steak and seafood. Please enjoy my offerings. I'm providing only a couple bites of everything so you can try it all. First, I have a Wedge Salad, a Caesar Salad, Cioppino, Navy Bean Soup and a Finger Food Platter." A platter of fried food, this could be bad. Fried food wins over everything else. Except his doesn't because it's greasy. The Wedge is geometric, but boring and tastes like the dressing came from a bottle. "For the entrees, I have a Rib eye Steak, a Pork Chop with Apricot Glaze, Shrimp and Grits, and Salmon. Sides can be ordered separately as the diner desires, I have Mashed Potatoes, Baked Potato, Steamed Vegetables, and Glazed Brussels Sprouts." The shrimp is overcooked, the pork chop is dry, and the cow is still mooing. The mashed potatoes have been overworked and the glaze on the Brussels sprouts tastes burnt. "For dessert, Homemade Vanilla Bean Ice Cream with a Chocolate Chip Cookie, Roasted Pears with Caramel, and Seasonal Cheesecake. Please enjoy."

"Thank you, Chef Clarke. Does anybody have any questions for Chef Clarke?" Katy turns to the crew and then to me.

Finally, James speaks up, "I'm concerned with food costs. We want the Supper Club to be accessible and affordable.

Typically a Rib eye steak would run upwards of $30 for the steak alone. Do you have an idea what the average meal would cost for a patron ordering dinner from your menu?"

Chef Clarke is caught a little off guard, "A steak dinner costs more everywhere. I'm guessing the average dinner would be about $50 for one person."

"Thank you Chef Clarke." James got his answer and looks to Katy.

"Alrighty then, Chef Clark you're dismissed. Thank you for allowing us to try your food." Chef Clarke leaves the room and Katy reminds everyone about their survey card, then surveys the plates and what's left on them. "Anybody have anything they would like to share about the tasting tonight?"

Archie and George both speak at exactly the same time, "It's not good." George laughs and Archie continues, "The shrimp is rubbery, the pork chop is dry, the glaze tastes burnt, the dessert doesn't make me want to order it, and overall it feels outdated."

George nods his head, "What he said."

"Okay, raise your hand if you prefer tonight's tasting over the comfort food last night." Katy scans the crew for a response and gives them a minute. No hands. "Please complete your survey cards and get them to me. Thank you." Katy turns to me, "Can I see you in my office?"

I follow her into her office and she locks the door behind us. "Obviously, Chef Danny has the best menu for the Supper Club. Is that going to be a problem for you or cause a problem having you both here?"

"No. It won't be a problem. I'm not going to lie, it will be nice to see each other and be in the same place. This is important to both of us and simply a coincidence that we're both getting what we want at the same time, in the same place. Besides, I'm only here on Saturday and he'll be in the kitchen."

I answer honestly, aware of how important this is and that I'm never lying again.

"Okay, I need to meet with the guys."

"Let me know if you need me. I'm going to hang with the band." I turn away and when I get to the stage I find the band is gone.

CHAPTER ELEVEN

The piano is sitting there, lonely. I sit down and feel the keys, running my fingers across them and playing some chord progressions. I start with Aerosmith's "I Don't Want to Miss a Thing," playing and singing like this is something I've done before, yet I've only ever done this with my keyboard and my headphones on in my own bedroom. I keep going with a series of Elton John, "Tiny Dancer," then "Someone Saved My Life Tonight," then "Your Song" and, finally, "Don't Let the Sun Go Down On Me." In fact, I played "Don't Let the Sun Go Down On Me" twice because of the adrenaline rush it sent through me. I have no idea how long I was alone there playing and singing, I had tuned everything around me out. When I finally look up, someone is walking toward me. Danny.

"Katy said I would find you here, but I didn't know you were the music." Danny stares at me in awe, "I never know what to expect from you, Jacks. I don't know why I'm surprised, you're amazing." Danny steps toward me with intent, but it's not a good idea and he reads the concern in my eyes.

"There are people here that we don't know and if we're going to work together, we'll need to be careful." I'm talking about the real world versus our world again and I hate it. Our world should be the real world. Someday it will be. "How long do you have until you start work?"

"I start my room service shift in an hour, but I'm only working until midnight. I had a schedule change since I'm starting my new chef gig tomorrow." Danny says this calmly and tries to keep a straight face.

I yell out, "Danny! I knew you would get it! I'm so proud of you! We need to celebrate."

"I'll see you at midnight, Jacks. I'm not going home tonight. I already called and told her I'm staying here because I'm working late and have to be at my new position early tomorrow."

I want to lean in close to him and tell him that I love him, hug him, kiss him, do everything I would do to congratulate him and show him how proud I am, but I can't because we're in public. I mouth words at him silently, "Want to go to my room and make-out? Probably nowhere safe to hide here."

Danny gets a wide grin, "I'd rather listen to you play."

"I'd love that." I move the piano bench, scoot over to make room and pat it for him to join me. He sits next to me, giving me a quick kiss on the cheek as he sits down and tries to keep his hands to himself. I gaze at him, trying to decide what to play and decide to start with Bon Jovi's "Always." His body language shows me he likes it, so I continue with "Don't Close Your Eyes" by Kix as I try to maintain the hard rock genre— Hey! Power ballads count. I keep going with "When I See You Smile" by Bad English and "I Live My Life For You" by Firehouse, paying attention to Danny's mood because I don't want to bore him. But, he's genuinely interested. I switch gears and do "If I Fell" by the Beatles, thinking about him and singing it to him, kinda corny, but sometimes you need to go with what you feel. I get an unexpected response from him, purely from the depth of desire in his eyes and go on with "In My Life."

At the end of the song, Danny gazes into my eyes, "I feel like I just attended your concert."

"Customized just for you." I say quietly with my heart beating out of my chest.

"Jackie, can I see you in my office. Chef, I'd like to see you, too." Katy calls out over the loud speaker.

There's nobody in the Club tonight besides the three of us and the guys might be hiding somewhere, but everyone else has moved on to Saturday night festivities. We walk into Katy's office and she shuts the door behind us. "Danny, we have a lot to work on tomorrow with the menu, food ordering, kitchen staff, and in addition to that the guys would like to feed everybody on the crew including the vocalists tomorrow at the mid point of the dress rehearsal, that should be about 1:30pm and there are about 35 of us. Also, we don't have any cooking staff on tomorrow, so it's all you."

"Would you rather I put out snacks, a variety of appetizers, a couple desserts and a warm main course that you can all munch on over a couple of hours and not have to stop dress rehearsal for food?" Danny offers another option.

"Yes. That's why you're the chef. You can do that by yourself and manage to prepare enough to feed all of us?"

"Of course. It's not enough notice to order food. I'll need to see what the kitchen has when the food order comes in tomorrow morning and work out a menu from there. Does that work for you, Katy?"

"Perfect. And, Jackie, the guys are impressed with the final set lists. They want you to know that you can still makes changes after the dress rehearsal if you want to. They appreciate your musical diversity and they don't know that you can play piano and sing yet. They want you here Friday morning through Sunday next weekend for final practices and to help get what we want out of the vocalists those first few shows. I already told them that you'll have to request time off and you need to keep your other job because one night a week isn't going to pay your bills. Tell your boss that we'll pay for his whole table of eight if you can have Friday off. Also, they want to be able to reach you, so here's your cell phone—Ms. Music Director. And, by the way, that title comes with a room at the Stardust whenever you want it until the Supper Club makes enough to support a full-time Music Director. You're always welcome to crash at my place, but I think you'd prefer to have some accessible privacy." Katy smiles at me knowingly, then at Danny and back at me.

"Music Director! Thank you, so much." I hug Katy and Danny's smile beams from ear to ear.

"I need to go work my room service shift, we'll celebrate later baby. Thank you, Katy. You two ladies should go out to dinner and celebrate. I'll meet you at midnight, Jacks." Danny disappears to go work room service for the last time.

"Katy, this is crazy!" I'm excited and can't contain it.

"The guys said they couldn't have done the job as well as you did. They told me to take you to dinner, too... so lets get out of here. I promise to have you back before midnight." Katy laughs as we walk through the casino.

Katy and I go to the coffee shop and have breakfast for dinner. We talk about the club and serving staff and the other vocalists. I don't ask about Kyle, she'll tell me when she's ready.

CHAPTER TWELVE

I get back to my room and have plenty of time to shower, wash off the make-up, and change into Danny's T-shirt before midnight. I turn on the hard rock station and review my copies of the set lists. I'm ready for tomorrow. I stop and think about the options for the addition of Janis to my set list, many of her songs were written and performed by other artists. I love "Piece of My Heart," but "Me and Bobby McGee" could be more Supper Club appropriate. I mean "Piece of My Heart" has a harder vibe to it, and "To Love Somebody" would be great, but the guys might think of it as the Bee Gees unless I sing it almost Joplin karaoke-like. Or maybe, I can sing it my way with a touch of Janis influence. I call Katy.

"Hello crazy person," she answers irritably.

"Hey, do you think I can try my Janis song for the guys in the morning before dress rehearsal? I have two and I want to let them pick."

"First, use your cell phone and I'll know it's you calling me. Second, I'm sure the guys would love to start the day with Janis. Third, stop working and get some rest. Tomorrow is going to be a long day and you have triple duty with performing, reviewing the vocalists, and practice after. Don't forget it's dress rehearsal, so you need to be here early for George and Marni. You should be ready before you sing for the guys, see you before 9am." Then Katy hangs up on me and my cell phone rings.

"Hello?"

"That's what it's like when your cell phone rings. Feel free to share the number. You can set an alarm on the phone and I'll be calling you whenever I want you, as will the guys. Goodnight." Katy hangs up on me again.

I call Dot on my new cell phone, give her the number, and tell her I'm Music Director. Then I repeat it with Jess. Both of them are excited for me and plan to come to the show soon.

I lie on the bed and wonder what George has in mind for me.

I wake up to Danny's lips on mine, tender open-mouthed kisses, and his hands gently holding my face to his. He pulls back and gazes at me, "You're perfect. I love that you can be made up and look hot, but then turn around and be bare for me. I know the real you is wearing my T-shirt and singing her heart out." He runs his hands down my body and takes a deep breath, before he simply puts his arms around me and holds me.

"We need to celebrate. We're both getting what we want and we get to do it in the same place."

Danny gets up and I watch him. He brought champagne, chocolate covered strawberries, and whipped cream. He pops the cork and pours two flutes of champagne. He hands me a glass and says, "To us," clinking our glasses together. We drink and feed each other the chocolate covered strawberries.

"What about the whipped cream? Shouldn't we be dipping the strawberries in it?" I ask him, anxious to dip into it since whipped cream is one of the best things on the planet.

Danny gives me a dirty grin, "That's for dessert."

I realize I better set my alarm or there is no way I will manage to get to the club by 9am. "Should we set you an alarm before we lose track?"

"Yea, food delivery is at 7am tomorrow and I need to be there. Nobody said getting what we want wasn't going to be work."

I set the alarms on my phone and make sure the volume is turned up. I look up from the phone and Danny attacks me with the whipped cream, smearing it on my lips and face. Kissing and licking me into a heated state of need. Suddenly I'm very aware of the fact that he's still dressed and I'm wearing only his T-shirt. I reach out and unbutton his jeans, while he pulls his shirt off. I touch his chest and run my finger along the tiger's back, then push down his jeans until they fall to the floor and he steps out of them. Danny pulls my shirt off, leaving me completely naked. His appreciation is obvious in his hooded eyes and ready cock. Standing in front of each other, face to face, I step closer and reach up to his lips, stretching to kiss him. Danny lifts me to his level and I wrap my legs around his waist. He takes us tumbling on to the bed, controlling our kiss like his life depends on it. His hard length is at my sex, wanting in. I move my hips encouraging him and he starts to push in, a little at a time, slowly, gently, deliberately, with controlled need. I can feel his blood racing with desire. The heat between us is palpable. He does his Danny thing, licking my lips so I'll open my mouth for him. He slides his tongue into my mouth. His hands on me, teasing my breasts and gliding across my body. He pushes deeper and deeper into me, stretching me and driving me to cry out, catching my cries with his mouth. His hands make my skin burn like I'm on fire. His kiss has taken over my whole world. His body is driving me into oblivion. I react primally, moving my hips and moaning. Touching his shoulders and upper arms, I'm entranced by the way his muscles move. Needing him unlike any man before. Needing him to give me my release. His slow, drawn out movements are different than before, torturously building to climax. He pushes into me and then pulls out, in and out, with unbelievable friction. "Please, Danny. Oh, Danny. Please." He starts to move quicker, but pulls out and moves to pay attention to my breasts while he lies between my legs. Squeezing my breasts and kissing my nipples, sucking hard on one and then the other. He sits up and appreciates my legs spread for him. He puts his hands under my ass and lifts me, so he can look at me. Danny lets out a sexual groan and dives into my wetness, licking and sucking at my hot and needy center. My body is on high alert and ready to explode at any second, he continues burying his face and maneuvers his tongue in deep. He sets me off and I cry out his name as I buck wildly. Danny moves quickly and pushes his huge cock all the way into me in one stroke. I scream out his name over and over as he pounds into me, and all I want is more.

His hot breath at my ear, his breathing ragged, and he whispers, "Say it, baby. I want to hear it while I'm inside you."

"I love you, Danny. It's only us, baby," in a sincere breathy tone that I didn't know I had in me.

Danny smiles and closes his eyes, "I love you, Jacks." His body shivers as he releases hard and curses silently. Danny reaches for my hand and intertwines our fingers. I pull the blankets up over us and we fall asleep in each other's arms.

———

6:30am comes early and the digital alarm, well it's alarming when you're not used to it. I wake up Danny, he kisses me, and gets up. Quickly getting cleaned up and dressed. "I'll be back before you get up, Jacks. Love you, babe," then I hear the door lock as it closes behind him.

I don't need much time to get ready. I stay in bed and fall

back to sleep, missing the warm body of my man and his arms around me protectively.

I hear the door open and Danny climbs back in bed with me, wrapping his arms around me and burying his nose in my hair. We sleep entangled until my alarm goes off. "Good morning, my sweet Jacks. I'm hoping this is the first of many Sundays that I wake up with you in my arms. We need to get up and go take over the world with music and food, to make sure that happens," Danny whispers sweetly in my ear.

"We got this, babe," I say without opening my eyes.

"Jacks!" Danny pulls the blankets away, always playing with me because I'm not a morning person. He laughs and I scream out playfully.

I get up and start singing as I walk around the room getting ready, still with Janis Joplin on my mind. "To Love Somebody" comes out with my own spin on it. I know George is going to dress me today, so I simply pull on black leggings, my suede boots and my faded out Guns n' Roses T-shirt. I tied my hair up wet last night, so I brush it out and blow-dry the part that's still damp. I gather a few things in a small bag and get ready to head down to the Supper Club.

"You look great just like that." Danny smiles and grabs me to give me a kiss.

"You appreciate my hard rock heart." I gaze at him with laughing eyes.

"You look good to me, no matter what. Always gorgeous. I'll ride down with you. I need to start prepping for lunch." Danny escorts me down to the casino floor. "Do you want coffee or anything? I can bring it to you when I bring the food over from the main kitchen."

"Katy has a coffeemaker, and she's in charge of donuts this morning. So, I'll be fine. Thank you, babe. Hey, no matter what today—you mean everything to me and I'm going to try not to make that obvious to everyone else." I turn and walk away toward the Supper Club happy. I can't believe that we're both getting what we want, more than I imagined possible.

CHAPTER THIRTEEN

I walk into the Supper Club and yell out, "Good Morning, Supper Club!" I get varying responses from different parts of the venue.

Katy calls out, "Coffee is ready and nobody has gotten to the donuts yet." I search out Katy and my morning needs.

"Good morning. Anything I need to know?" I ask her happily.

"Seriously? Wipe that satisfied grin off your face or I'm not sharing donuts." Katy glares at me as she reads my face.

"What? It's not like I had an all night marathon or anything." Katy gives me a dirty look. "Fine, I'll keep it to myself. Now, what can I do?" I ask as I pour a cup of coffee and snatch the yellow cake donut with chocolate icing and peanuts on it.

"The other vocalists will start wandering in soon, so you need to go see George and be ready first. Where's the chef this morning?"

"Danny went to the main kitchen to get the food for today. He went in early and took what he wanted when the delivery came in earlier. He should be in the kitchen here anytime."

"What's he making?" Katy asks about lunch.

"I don't know. I didn't ask. I'm sure it's something good. Everything he makes is good." I smile as I remember exactly what he does so well and laugh to myself.

Katy rolls her eyes at me in disgust, "Go. Just, go."

"George, I'm coming for you!" I call out as I walk into wardrobe.

"Finally, I've been waiting for you." George examines me up and down, then shakes his head. "What is this you're wearing? I know you always wear the boots, but leggings and a T-shirt?"

"I decided not to worry about it because you're going to dress me anyway."

"True. Okay, then let's get you dressed. I have four options for you." George holds up four different outfits on hangers and waits for my reaction.

"I'm not a big fan of skirts on stage. I don't like long skirts and I feel like the crowd is looking up my skirt when it's short." George puts two of the outfits on the rack.

"Which of these two are you going with today?" George waits for me to choose.

"What do the shoes look like?"

"Option one you wear your suede boots. Option two you wear chunky high healed booties." George didn't even wait for me to answer and handed me option one. "Everything you need is on the hanger. Come back to me when you're dressed for accessories and Marni. Robyn, Jackie's going to need you to tape her up."

I take a good look at the hanger of clothes and realize it's a dress. A long button-up shirt style that cinches with a belt at the waist. Like a long men's dress shirt. The shirt is light grey and I decide to leave my black leggings on underneath it with my boots. The shirt has been tailored to fit me and the sleeves have been removed, as well as the top four buttons. There is a scarf, but no belt and I assume the scarf is meant to take the place of the belt. The scarf is black with silver sequins. Robyn tapes up my breasts and arranges the outfit, adjusting the location of the scarf, changing the knot, unbuttoning the shirt another notch, flaring out the collar. She gapes at my leggings and doesn't say a word. I go back to George and await judgment.

George makes a face when he sees me, "I guess the leggings aren't bad with the dress. What's this here? I don't remember you having freckles on your breast here."

I look down thinking that I don't have freckles and realize I've got hickeys. "Um, yeah. No, I don't have freckles." I blush and wait because judgment is coming.

George examines closer, "Oh, well somebody had fun last night. Marni, Jackie needs concealer on her boobs." He gives me another once over, "I'll bring some accessories over to you at make-up."

Marni sits me in her chair, "Touching up your cleavage was not on my list of top ten things I wanted to do today," she glares at me irritably, but then changes her tone. "However, I do appreciate a good sex story." Marni smiles at me like she's waiting for the sordid story as repayment and continues her process of making me stage ready.

I think about what I can tell Marni. I mean, obviously I can't tell her who or anything like that, but that doesn't mean I can't give her something. "I've been seeing this guy for awhile and he met me at my room last night with champagne to celebrate. Nothing crazy."

Marni stops, "You're going to have to give me more than that."

"The score was three for me and one for him." Trying to keep it clean.

"Keep going." Marni shakes her head like she's pulling teeth.

"He's got a great package and knows how to get things done. And, you might have noticed he has a talented mouth. Better?" I work for approval and dismissal from the conversation.

Marni shifts on her feet and stares into the mirror at me, pointing down and silently asking if he went down on me. I catch her eyes with mine in the mirror and nod with a sated smile on my face. "Girl! He was all over you." That seemed to do the trick and she was back focused on the job at hand. She called over George as she put the finishing touches on my make-up, "Georgie, what are you thinking for her hair with this outfit?"

George examines me, spins me around. "I kind of like the long tousled look she has going on. Maybe get control of the wave a bit and clean up the look?"

Marni nods and goes to work on my hair, leaving me with long loose waves, my hair parted over to the side and hanging in my face. She finishes my hair with her magic potion for making hair shiny. I turn to George, "I really do prefer jeans and suede. I love the look overall and I look amazing. But, it doesn't feel like me."

Marni glares at George knowingly, "You're beautiful. We will find the perfect look for you. You need to look respectable today when they introduce you to the other vocalists. They aren't going to like having one of their peers being in charge of the music, Ms. Music Director."

"Maybe I should look tougher today, so they don't get any ideas?"

"Trust me, you don't need help being tough. You've got this. Show them all what you've got and make sure you're last on the list to sing today. They don't need to know you're one of the singers until they have to." George makes a good point and Marni agrees with him.

"You guys rock! I need to go find the schedule for today. Thank you." I take off to find Katy.

"Katy, can I have a copy of the schedule for today?"

"Sure." Katy hands me the schedule and I'm scheduled to sing in the middle of the list.

"Can you move me to the end, please?" Katy turns to me, wanting more. "I'm thinking that I'm their peer and Music Director. Better for them not to know I'm singing until the end, gives me more credibility."

"No problem. Do you think you can find the kitchen and make sure the chef has chocolate on the lunch table? I need a fix. Also, the guys are here and can hear you whenever you want, just start singing."

"Yes, ma'am."

I find the Supper Club kitchen and the new hot chef working away. "Chef?"

Danny turns to me and smiles, "Music Director."

"Katy needs a chocolate fix and wants to make sure there is chocolate on the lunch menu. Do you have anything I can take to her, to keep her happy?"

Danny laughs, "I just put chocolate cupcakes in the oven. You can take her the bowl to lick or she'll have to wait for lunch."

I dial Katy's number and she answers, "I know you're busy, but I have a bowl with chocolate cake batter…" Katy hangs up on me.

Katy comes walking into the kitchen, "Bowl please." She snatches it away from me and I decide it's best to let her have it if I want to keep all of my fingers today.

"Ladies, you're both beautiful. Get out of my kitchen. I have work to do and no help, so no time for distractions." Danny gestures for us to leave him to his zone. Katy takes the bowl with her back to her office and I hear the door slam behind her. I head to the stage in search of Archie.

"Hey Archie! Are you and the band ready for today?" I ask very upbeat.

"We're ready. Any changes?"

"The guys want me to add a Janis song to my set and I want to sing two of them for them and let them pick. Does the band know 'To Love Somebody' and 'Me and Bobby McGee?'"

"Are you sure you need us? There's a rumor you play piano."

"That's not my place here. I'm a singer."

Archie nods, appreciating that I respect the band. "We know those songs. But, you're going to have to do a song for us solo on the piano first." Grinning at me with the upper hand.

"You got it. Any requests?" I turn to the band, waiting for their response.

The drummer speaks up, "I heard you played 'Don't Let the Sun Go Down on Me' and I love that one," he surveys the other band members and there's some silent, approving communication between then.

I walk over to the piano and loosen up a bit, playing a scale and humming. Then I confidently start in on the piano intro and begin the vocals steady and even, letting the intensity build slightly as I reach the chorus. The band joins in, one by one during the second verse starting with drums and plays through to the end with me. Gradually building until I hit a climax at the end of the song. There's hooting, hollering, and applause coming from all over the club. The band stays quiet and Archie has a stern expression on his face, "So, it's true. You can play and Katy was right, you're great." Each band member reaches out to give me a high five as I get up from the piano and move to the mic at center stage.

"Can we do 'To Love Somebody' and tone it down a bit from the Janis version, but keep it more up than the Bee Gees?

I want to try something a little bit different." I ask Archie, hoping for a suggestion.

Archie counts the band down and they start in. I bring the vocals in breathy and tender, then open up for the chorus. I bring it back down to my standard voice for the remaining verses and try to project the emotion of the song, taking the last verse up an octave and belting the last chorus. I bring it back down at the end and finish the song out free styling my vocals. I turn to Archie for approval of my arrangement and get a thumbs up. "Guys, that's the first Janis option and here is the second." I turn to Archie and he walks to the front of the stage bringing a stool. He starts in on acoustic guitar and I conjure the singer-songwriter inside me for "Me and Bobby McGee." It's invigorating, only the two of us. "James and Kyle, please let me know if you have a preference for my set." I turn to Archie and the band, "You guys are all great. Thanks for backing me up."

I check in with Katy to find that Kyle is in her office again, but this time he appears to be working and not wrapped around her. "Hey, how long until we're going to get started?"

"The vocalists are in wardrobe, we can get started as soon as they're done." Katy checks time, "I'm going back there to check on them now, they should be done. I need to make sure they're all here."

"Okay, so I have five minutes to disappear?" I ask, hoping because I need walk off my adrenaline from being on stage.

"You got it. Don't mess yourself up. Remember, dress rehearsal."

"Yes, ma'am."

I stick my head into the kitchen, "I'm going for a walk out to the casino, need anything chef?"

"What are you looking for?" Danny asks.

"I need a soda." I admit my addiction.

"I've got Dr. Pepper for you right here in the refrigerator, and water." Funny that being in the same room with him somehow calms me. He points to the refrigerator with the soda and keeps working. "You let me know what you want and I'll make sure it's here."

There's no one in the kitchen except us, I walk near him as I'm leaving the kitchen and speak quietly, "You're already here and I don't want anything else." My adrenaline contained, my addiction satisfied and my heart happy.

CHAPTER FOURTEEN

I meet up with Katy in wardrobe to check on how things are coming along and find her trying to wrangle the vocalists. It's an odd sight since Katy is always in control. She stops suddenly and changes her tone, "Ladies, you need to sign in with me immediately to get your copy of the dress rehearsal schedule. You will need to stay through the whole rehearsal and may need to stay for an additional practice afterward. You need to be ready and waiting when it's your turn. I will not think twice about cutting you. In fact, line up here so I can make sure you're all here." Now that's Katy. The singers line up shoulder to shoulder. George and Marni join me to watch, we discuss each of the ladies and how they responded to them. I remind George to keep the show in mind and make sure they appear fabulous even if they're a bitch, and we laughed. Katy lines them up in the order they will be performing and decides to get started. The ladies are instructed to sit at the tables in the audience and Katy drags me out on to the stage. "Ladies and gentlemen! It's time for the dress rehearsal. I have a couple of announcements to get us started. This is Jackie and she has been named Music Director for the Supper Club."

Katy claps. "The Supper Club Chef will be Chef Danny and he's preparing lunch for you today." Approving noises come from different locations in the club. "Lastly, this is the Archies. Appreciate them. They are the best band in Las Vegas and we're lucky to have them. Now, let's get on with it!"

Katy and I make our way to the table where we find the guys already planted, while the stage crew takes over. Katy has a timer and takes notes on things that don't go as smoothly as they should and times when there is silence. I have my schedule for the day and the set lists. I'm watching how the vocalists move and that they stick to their set list in order, no changing songs or arrangements. Making notes on songs that need work and set lists that are lacking something.

Danny walks out pushing a cart full of food, and sets up the table with different platters and bowls, leaving everything covered. Then he brings Katy, the guys, and I our lunches already plated and looking delicious. I drool at the large plate in front of me, the thick piece of Lasagna plated with extra sauce over the top, Mixed Greens Salad with Danny's Balsamic Vinaigrette, and Garlic Toast. Then he sets a crudité plate with freshly made hummus at the center of the table. Next he places a small plate in front of each of us with a cheesecake cream-filled chocolate cupcake that's topped with ganache, a warm chocolate chip cookie, whipped cream, and a strawberry. "Katy, I hope this is what you had in mind. All of this is available on the table I've set up, so the crew can take what they want. As well as, ice bins with water and soda. Can I get you anything else?"

The guys look at the food and then each other. Katy turns to me and I already have the cupcake in my mouth. "It looks delicious, chef. Thank you," Katy approves.

"Thank you. Please let me know if I can get you anything else or if you have any feedback. I want the food to be exactly what you want. Enjoy." Danny turns and goes to take the covers off the food on the table he had set up.

I sit there with basically the whole cupcake in my mouth and again think about how I'm going to need to get a gym membership, but it's so worth it. Katy shakes her head at me, "Can't you be normal and eat your dessert last?"

"What if I get full? Dessert is more important. I can't leave chocolate sitting there lonely." I scoop up some of the whipped cream with the cookie and I'm in heaven. Katy is meticulous, trying everything in the order it should be eaten. Very proper. Then going back and eating everything on her plate.

The rehearsal is going well overall, no big snafus. Timing is close. The ladies and the band are playing the songs in the correct order with no glaring mistakes. We're getting near the end of the dress rehearsal and I know I'm next. I make notes on the vocalist before me quickly and head to the stage, not wanting to throw off the timing. I high-five every member of the band as I walk onto the stage and tell them they're doing an awesome job. Archie gives me a nod and I move to the mic at center stage. I look out at the audience, surveying the scene. Katy has invited Danny out of the kitchen, he's sitting in my seat at the table with Katy and the guys with a plate of cupcakes, cookies, and whipped cream. Archie gets the band started and my set is in motion. After watching the other vocalists all day, I've learned that I want to move around and try not to be stiff—that's no fun to watch. The confidence I've gained being here this weekend, the camaraderie of working with the band and the trust they have placed in me making me Music Director, all make me better. I feel how much I've progressed since I arrived here Thursday. Four days of my life that might have the biggest impact on my career. I sing without worry. I take liberties with the music that I've only ever taken in the privacy of my bedroom. When I need emotion, I focus on Danny. I'm not afraid. I'm going to get what I want. The other vocalists will respect me. At the end of my set, the table stands and applauds, including Danny who is noticeably proud of me. Danny returns to the kitchen and Katy joins me on stage.

"Not bad overall, ladies. Timing was good. Kudos to our Music Director for the set list choices." Katy passes the mic to me.

"Ladies, I'd like to meet with all of you together. Please hang out and I'll be down there shortly. Thank you." I make my way down to the tables and gather the singers around one table. "I think you all did a good job today. I've made some notes on each of your set lists. I need some of you to move more on stage. I need some of you to change out a song or two on your set list, in a couple cases the set overall needs some more oomph. I need some of you to work on a song or two, that's not quite up to performance quality. I've also written my phone number on your set list. Review your notes. I want each of you to call me and leave me your phone number. I'll be reaching out to you to chat individually. Thank you for your hard work today." I wait around because I know they're going to read their notes and have questions, but they all kind of stare at me questioningly and then leave. I'm okay with that.

CHAPTER FIFTEEN

This is when I start to have an emotional breakdown. The weekend has been almost perfect. The opportunity is more than I ever wished for. I have new friends. I'm in Vegas with Danny, working in the same place, and I have a room right here in the hotel. Everything is going so well. I woke up two of the last three days in Danny's arms. I've grown musically and what performance fears I had are gone. It's truly been an amazing weekend, an unforgettable experience. Now, I have work in the morning and I need to pack up and drive home. It's late Sunday afternoon. My warehouse sales job starts early tomorrow morning and I better be early to make up for my Friday hours, especially if I have any hope of getting next Friday off. I don't want to leave. I don't want this perfect weekend to end. What if it's a dream and when I wake up at home in the morning it didn't really happen? No, I don't want to leave. I don't want to leave Danny, I want to keep seeing him everyday. I want to keep sneaking my Danny time in whenever we can. I want the baby steps that we get to have on the path to our someday. I'm not okay with this.

I walk into Katy's office and close the door behind me. "Am I clear until Friday morning?"

"I believe so, if I need anything I'll call you and I'm sure that I'll call you. Let me know as soon as you get approval to have Friday off."

"I will. I plan to drive back to Vegas on Thursday after work. Thank you for everything. I appreciate you, Katy." Katy gives me a wink and a high-five. "What time is Chef scheduled until today?"

"I think he's working on clean up. We're going to be busy the next few days with menus and things. He should probably take a break or go home for the night."

"I may take advantage of that 'break' before I leave to drive home." I wave goodbye as I leave her office and head into the kitchen to find Danny.

"Hey are you done with clean up? Katy says you should take a break or get out of here for the night." I find Danny working at a table making notes in the middle of the kitchen with dishwashers running.

Danny glances up, "Hey beautiful, I'm just finishing up a basic list of kitchen necessities I need here."

"I need to go get packed up and drive home to LA tonight. I have work in the morning. Would you like to join me for a bit before I go?" I gaze at Danny with big eyes, full of intent.

"Yes. Please. Go on up and get packed. I'll be up in a few." Danny smiles and the flames flare up in his eyes.

I turn to leave and he catcalls me as I'm walking out of the kitchen. It makes me happy all over and my cheeks warm. I go to wardrobe and change back into my T-shirt, then back to my room to pack. I don't remember this journey to my room from the Supper Club being so sad, and why does this elevator ride seem to take forever? I try to focus on the task at hand and that I have things to get done so I can be back here Thursday night.

Laundry doesn't do itself, I have bills to pay, Joe needs me to do sales, I need a manicure, and I need to go shopping.

I walk into my room and find the remnants of last night, an empty champagne bottle, strawberry tops, a bed that has been slept in, and a dirty room because room service is waiting for me to check out. I sit down on the bed, pull my boots off and lay my head down as I survey the room for what I have to pack. The pillow smells of Danny and suddenly tears are rolling down my face. It's stupid. We can't be together all the time or even every night. I mean, I have to be a secret. It's not fair, but his little Jackie needs him too. He's going to have a busy few days doing menu prep and working with his kitchen staff. He doesn't need me to be a distraction. That's it, focus and be strong. You can do this. You'll be back here in only four days. Danny and the Supper Club will be waiting for you. I get up and turn up the hard rock station, then I wander my room tossing everything dirty into my dirty clothes bag. I gather the clothes and accessories from George in a neat pile. I set my flip-flops by the door and take a minute to wash my face, removing the make-up that's been destroyed by my tears.

Danny walks through the door as I'm putting the last of my things in my bags. Without words, he reads the expression on my face, walks to me with an urgency and embraces me. Taking control of the world and everything around us while he can. Making it all disappear. Sheltering me from the real world and taking us both away from reality. He puts his lips on mine, taking what he wants with an urgent need. Sucking on my tongue and feeling my breasts through my T-shirt. It runs through me like lightning and I grind against him, driving a needy sound from both of us. Danny backs me to the bed and pulls my shirt off as he whispers in my ear in a deep, out of breath voice, "I need you, Jacks. I want to make you mine."

"I'm already yours, Danny." I manage to squeak out as he

kisses my neck. He hooks his fingers in my leggings and panties, pulling them both off at once and leaving me naked. I reach to pull his shirt off, but can't do it, "Off." His shirt disappears, revealing his tiger tattoo and I'm drawn to kiss his chest. His pecs and strong arms, taught and hard. He reaches between my legs, cupping me with his hand, dragging his fingers across my sensitive folds. He claims my mouth with his, making a silent statement that I belong to him and no one else can have me. He slides his finger in, stroking me a few times before adding a second finger and all I can think is that I want more, I want all of him. "Please Danny, I want all of you." The request makes his heart beat faster and he loses his pants. He sits back and lifts my left foot into the air, kissing my ankle open mouthed. I reach for Tiger and Danny moves closer to me, laying his hard length on me while he continues to kiss my leg and make his slow journey. Lying on my back in bed, Tiger reaches from my sex to my navel. The size and the weight of him is bared for me, he's bigger than I remember and completely solid as a rock. I run my fingers down his length, then wrap my hand around him as far as I can reach and hold him. Danny moves back to my ankle that he's holding straight up in the air and kisses it as he pulls back and pushes Tiger into me. I'm immediately thrown into an ethereal state and at Danny's mercy, crying out his name.

"I've got you Jacks, I promise I'll always take good care of you." He pushes into me farther and farther, stretching me like a custom glove meant just for him. Pushing and pushing until I scream out, then he holds still and kisses my ankle. He lifts my right leg and puts his mouth on it, kissing and licking from my ankle to my knee, then back to the left leg for the same treatment, while he slowly moves in and out. He runs his hands down my legs to my ass, lifting and grabbing my ass, pulling me to him as he bends toward my mouth to kiss me, taking my feet with him and folding me in half as he licks across my lips, kissing me passionately. His focus on my mouth and our kiss, he pulls my attention to his mouth on mine and his lips, every movement of his tongue, every suck and nibble at my lip. It feels like heaven when he starts moving inside me again. Pushing into me as far as he can, taking me deeper than before with my feet pinned at my ears. He starts to move quicker and with urgency, "Jacks. I need... to.... Jacks, you're so tight around me. I swear... I..." I know what he likes best and reach to touch myself, but I don't need to. He pounds into me hard and my body rocks uncontrollably into his, bucking wildly with his, meeting his strokes because we were made for each other. I scream out his name as I grasp at his hard cock inside me, tightening around him as he gets harder and starts to throb. My body is on fire and flaring up with every stroke. His body relaxes all over as he slowly releases my legs and puts his arms around me, holding me tight against him. "Jacks baby, I'm never letting you go again." His heart beat comes back down and his breathing finds it's way back to normal. I feel the same way. I'm never letting him go.

I don't want this time with Danny to end. I don't want to drive home to LA. But, this is a temporary situation and I need to be an adult. I need to do the responsible thing and get home, so I can be at work early in the morning. I mean, Joe really has been lenient by allowing me the time off and I want more time off and most likely will need even more time off. I need to do my part, too. It's already going to be after 10pm before I get home. I need to go. "Danny, I need to drive home tonight. I don't want to leave you."

Danny sighs deeply, "I know, I understand. I need to go home to my Jackie, too. But, I don't want to leave you."

"It's only four days, right? That's nothing compared to the time we were apart. And, we know it's going to get better." I smile at Danny and show my heart. He can probably see it flopping around like a squirmy little puppy on it's back, showing it's soft underbelly.

"Yeah. It will get better. You know they're going to want you here full-time soon. I could hear the dress rehearsal today and none of the other vocalists came near you. They need you to sing every night and handle the music. Besides, the place is going to be busy with all the diners checking out the new chef," Danny chuckles to himself.

"That's the right attitude. We're going to rock this place!" I get up, put my clothes on and do a double check around the room to make sure I haven't missed anything. The only thing I haven't packed is Danny and that's not an option. Then I notice a box on the dresser, "What's in the box?"

"It's for you. Nothing special, just a care package to help you get through the next few days." Danny says as he pulls on his clothes and picks up my bags. "Let's go."

We leave the room and I realize that I won't be able to hug him or kiss him once we hit the casino floor. His hands are full with my stuff, so I take advantage of the situation. I stretch up to kiss him and snake my arms around his neck, running my fingers through his hair until the elevator dings and the doors open. I step back and walk out to my truck with him like he's only a co-worker. After all, we do work at the same place and I do appreciate not having to carry my bags. I thank Danny for carrying my bags and make sure he has my cell phone number as I climb into my truck.

"I'll call you from my kitchen, since I have a phone line now. Drive safe, baby. I love you, Jacks." Danny starts to walk away, but turns back to me. "Babe, I know this is strange because I have to hide you, but when I say it's only you I mean I won't be with anybody else and I don't want you to. Now, please check in with Dot and let her know you're on your way home. I want to know somebody is watching out for you." Danny turns away and walks back to the Stardust. I enjoy the view, he sees me checking him out when he turns around and waves getting a grin on his face. I call Dot quickly to check in and hit the road. I love that man and how he had to make sure I'm confident about how he feels and what he wants. Nobody compares to him. I learned the hard way. I'm never letting him go again, either.

CHAPTER SIXTEEN

The drive home helped me clear my head. Of course, I'm always happy when I'm speeding with the windows down and the radio blaring. I make a mental list of all the things I need to get done before I drive back to Vegas and all the things I want to get done before I drive back to Vegas. They sound like the same thing, but they really aren't. I want to make myself better and that means I need to scour the warehouse in the morning and find the songs I want to practice. I want to show up wearing clothes that will be found acceptable, so George doesn't ask me what I'm wearing and Katy doesn't send me to wardrobe. I want to learn a song from my set well enough to perform on the piano. I need to do laundry. I need a manicure. I need to work my ass off at the warehouse. I need to talk to Joe about Friday. Most of all, I need Danny and, no, Danny shouldn't be classified as a want.

I pull into my apartment complex, relieved to be home and ready to go to bed. Hoping that I don't have anyone waiting for me at my door, so I can toss a load of laundry in the washer, check in with Dot, and crash for the night. I pull into my parking space and Bryan is waiting for me. There went sleep, or maybe not, I can make this work. I get out of my truck, "Hey, Bryan! Can you help me unload?" Bryan walks over and grabs my bags for me while I unlock the door to my apartment. "Thanks. So, what's up?" I give Dot a quick call to tell her I'm home and continue my conversation with Bryan.

"I was worried about you. You never came home from work last Thursday and I haven't heard from you." Bryan doesn't sound happy, in fact his tone is leaning more toward irritated than worried.

"Sorry, I didn't even think about it. Katy called me and the guys needed me at the Supper Club Thursday afternoon. I got Joe to give me the days off and the guys provided a room for me at the Stardust. It's been the most amazing weekend."

"The guys? Who's Katy? I bet the guys got you a room, they probably wanted something." Shaking his head, Bryan follows me around my apartment while I put things away and try to get my laundry sorted out.

"Katy is assistant to the guys and way cool, love her to pieces. We went out and partied on the strip Friday night. The guys are the two guys in charge of the Supper Club, kind of creators, directors, and producers all in one or I should say all in two. The guys are not at all interested in me for anything other than my musical talent, so don't be like that." I give Bryan the evil eye and shoot down his attitude.

I find my care package as I'm unpacking and open it to discover the delights that were packed for me. Proof that Danny loves me: three chocolate cupcakes with the cheesecake cream filling and ganache, two chocolate dipped strawberries, and a dozen chocolate chip cookies. It smells delectable and I want to eat it all.

"What the fuck was that? You look like you just had an orgasm." Fuck! I really need to get control of that. Bryan glares at me with confusion, like I'm losing my mind.

First, I don't want to share. Second, I don't want to tell him because then I'll have to share. Third, I don't want to show him because then I'll have to share. "What are you talking about? Are you sex crazed or something?" I turn it back around on him. Ha! Now, I need to pivot the conversation. "So, you're never going to believe this. The Supper Club named me Music Director. It's so exciting! I chose the set lists for all of the performing vocalists and the whole shebang. I sang with the band. George and Marni, I mean wardrobe and make-up made me gorgeous everyday. Truly a crazy amazing four days and I'm going back Thursday night, but I need to get Joe to give me Friday off."

"Wow! Music Director? Seriously? That's a big step. What does it pay?" Bryan asks too many questions.

"For now, it provides me a room while I'm there and I honestly don't know what the pay is for any of it. It really doesn't matter because I love it. You should hear my Beatles Medley, the band meshed it all together perfectly without a single awkward pause or transition." I'm interrupted by my cell phone ringing. "Hello?"

"Hey this is Katy. Did you make it home?"

"Yea, just got here."

"I want to make sure you have the contact info for all of the singers, so I'm emailing that to you as well as the final set lists. George showed us the photos they took of you styled and they're great, I'll email those to you as well," Katy is being all work and in charge.

"Great. I forgot to drop off the clothes back with George, I hope that's not a problem. I'll bring them back Thursday night."

"Not at all, don't try to wash them or anything. George will have a different wardrobe ready for you anyway. Also, I like having you around here. It was great having another chick here to hang with."

"Thanks, Katy. Are we going out this weekend or is it going to be too busy?"

"I like the way you think. How about Thursday night? Saturday we'll all be celebrating opening night."

"It's on! I'll get there as early as I can on Thursday. See you then," and Katy hangs up.

Bryan is watching and listening to everything in awe, no clue what to think. I immediately go to my computer to check my email and Bryan looks over my shoulder at the photos of me professionally styled.

"Who's that? And, when did you get a cell phone?" Still too many questions.

"Cell phone goes with the Music Director gig. That's me, you idiot! Professionally styled by wardrobe and make-up, stage ready. What do you think?" My confidence and attitude are evident.

"Well, you're always beautiful. That's a little over the top I think or maybe not enough of a top. Everybody doesn't need to see that much of you. Opening night is Saturday?"

"Yes and I think I look hot. So does everybody else."

"Is opening night sold out yet?" Bryan asks and I'm not sure I like it.

I shrug my shoulders and ring Katy to find out about seats for opening night. There are limited seats left and she gives me the number to call if people want to reserve seats, which I pass on to Bryan. I never considered that he'd actually go to my show, he always has gigs on the weekend. Danny, Bryan, Joe, Dot, Jess, and everybody else in the same place, awkward.

"So, anyway I gotta get some sleep." Hint, hint, get out. Bryan follows me into my bedroom. Not hint, hint, come fuck me! I walk back to the door and open it for him.

"Really? You're kicking me out?" Bryan looks butt hurt.

"Yes. I've got a ton to do and a short amount of time to do it. Thanks for stopping by." Bryan gives me the strangest glare of confusion and leaves without questioning it. Relieved, I lock the door, change into Danny's T-shirt and of course my phone rings. "Hello?"

"Hey Jacks, just wanted to make sure you got home and she's out tonight, so I'm taking advantage. Are you home and everything is fine?"

I smile and my whole body is happy, "I'm home and everything is fine. I have this box of chocolate that this hot guy made for me, too."

"Wow! You must be special. Tell me about this hot guy." Danny is playing with me and I decide to play along.

"Well, his ass looks so fucking hot in his Levi's, he's hung like a horse and he knows how to use it, I love his blonde shaggy hair, he has chocolate brown eyes that just melt me, he has this really sexy tiger tattoo on his chest, and I'm going to have to join a gym because he's such a good cook. But most importantly, he makes me laugh and I love spending time with him. I think we're in love."

"Do you really think all of those things about me?" Danny is suddenly serious.

"Yes. It's all the truth. Nobody makes me feel the way that you do." I'll tell him everything. I'm never lying to him again, no matter what.

"Be confident and know we're in love, Jacks. I've never been there before and I'm happy that I'm there with you." Jackie walks in to find her Daddy and I listen to her sweet voice. "I only have a minute. Jackie needs me."

"Go be with your girl. Also, ask Katy for the photos of me when you're at the Supper Club tomorrow. You'll love them. I'm wiped out and just climbed in bed. Good night, Danny."

"Love you, babe," and he hangs up.

Okay, that was the best thing that could've happened tonight. Now, sleep with dreams of Danny.

CHAPTER SEVENTEEN

I wake up early Monday morning and start my mission. I pull on my ripped jeans, my Aerosmith T-shirt, and my Reeboks. I tie my hair up in a knot, change my laundry, and stop to pick up donuts on my way to work.

I'm inspired by my T-shirt today and keep finding myself singing Aerosmith. I walk into the office singing "Cryin'" at the top of my lungs and walk into Joe's office giving him first choice of the donuts. I leave the donuts in the break room and Joe calls out, "So, it must've been a good trip to Las Vegas?"

I walk back into his office, "It was amazing. If you'll be so kind as to give me this Friday off, the Supper Club will cover the cost of your whole table of eight." Joe looks at me, foreseeing the need for more and more time off. "Joe, they made me the Music Director. They want me there for the final run-through on Friday and you know we open on Saturday. They gave me a cell phone, I'll make sales calls Friday morning and work on sales for you from Vegas. I'll go visit our Vegas customers in person. I don't expect you to pay me for the time, only my sales. Please, Joe."

"Sing something for me while I think about it." It's still early and nobody else is in the building.

I stare at Joe, "May I play the piano in the warehouse?"

Joe glares at me unsure, "Yea."

"I'll leave the door to the warehouse open, so you can hear," I turn and walk out into the warehouse. I uncover the high gloss ebony grand piano and open the lid. I sit down and warm up for a few minutes while I consider what I want to sing for Joe. I start with my current hang up and play "I Don't Want to Miss a Thing," singing loudly to make sure Joe can hear me. I finish the song and get no response, so I keep going, thinking Elton John might be more impressive with "Someone Saved My Life Tonight." Still nothing. I remember singing for Danny and play a few Beatles tunes, "If I Fell," then "Blackbird," and finally "In My Life," and I listen.

I hear shuffling around in the warehouse and Joe calls out showing no emotion, "Do another Elton John." I do as requested and hit "Don't Let the Sun Go Down On Me" hard. I finish the song to cheering and clapping from Joe and all of my co-workers. I turn to find them all standing behind me. Joe walks over to me with a proud grin and puts his hand on my shoulder, "Jackie has been named the Music Director for a new venue in Las Vegas called the Supper Club. She'll be working away from the warehouse some days. I have two tables reserved for opening night this Saturday and would like you all to join me. As you all heard, I think the show will be great and she deserves our support." I stand up and hug Joe. "Now, play one more to get us back to work and get to work, you've got lots to get done if you're making up for days missed."

"Yes, sir!" I sit down at the keyboard and continue with Elton John's "Tiny Dancer." Then I get to work, needing to follow up on sales and check in with my stores to review what they've sold over the weekend. I have an idea about taking

CDs to Vegas with me that feature songs from the Supper Club set list, but I need to talk to Katy about that.

I call Katy on my break, "Hello, it's too early."

"Good morning, ma'am." I laugh, "You aren't fooling me, I know you're at the club."

"Whatever. Any updates?"

"Yes, I'm off Friday and will be there Thursday probably before 8pm. Um, have you considered selling CDs at the Supper Club?" I ask cautiously.

"Like what? You have something in mind?"

"I'm not sure. I thought CDs with the same style of music, including some of the songs on the set lists might generate a few extra bucks for the club."

"I hadn't thought about it, but we've been recording all the performances. I guess we could make a CD to sell, but I don't know what the guys will think about that. Interesting." I can hear her wheels turning.

"All of the performances on stage have been recorded?"

"Yea, you didn't know?"

"I had no idea. Also, I need to know what hours you're going to need me this weekend. I made a deal with my boss that I would do some sales while I'm in Vegas."

"I'll email the schedule to you this afternoon. I'm working on finalizing it this morning as soon as I'm done working with the chef."

"Are you with Danny right now?"

"Yea, we're working on menu design, food order, food costs, choosing sous chefs and line cooks... all that wonderful kitchen stuff. He has most of it already set, but the guys want to approve the pricing on the menu and Danny needs to decide who he wants working in his kitchen within his budget."

"If you hang out with him too much, you'll have to join the gym with me." I laugh, "I know he has been working on it and keeping notes on things. I think he knows what he's doing and is more than a good cook."

"I'd say you're biased, but I agree with you. He's making my job easy."

"I have to get back to work. Tell my man hi for me," and I hang up.

Somehow I manage to get through the rest of the day focused. Tuesday and Wednesday fly by, but I manage to get caught up before I leave the warehouse on Thursday and Joe let me skip lunch and leave early for Vegas. I had so much to do this week and, well at least I got my laundry done. Maybe I can get a manicure and do some shopping when I get to Vegas. I listen to my new Janis Joplin Greatest Hits on my drive and find myself playing "Piece of My Heart" on repeat.

CHAPTER EIGHTEEN

I pull into a parking space at the Stardust at 6pm and I've either been speeding or found a way to bend the space-time continuum. I never make the drive to Vegas that quickly. I hop out of my truck and go directly to the club, still singing "Piece of My Heart."

I step into the Supper Club and everything seems pretty quiet. I lean in the doorway of Katy's office, "Honey, I'm home!"

Katy laughs and hands me an envelope with room keys, "I have a few more hours of work to do. Let's go out a little later, jeans and T-shirt night. Go say hi to your boy toy and get settled in your room."

"I like a jeans and T-shirt place. I want to go shopping and get a manicure. Find me when you're ready to go out." I turn to visit the kitchen.

"Wait. I want to go shopping and get a manicure. Give me forty-five minutes and come get me."

Katy surprises me, "Isn't that going to make it too late?"

"This is Vegas. There is plenty of time." She smiles and shoos me out of her office.

I gaze into the kitchen and check out a hot blonde guy wearing blue jeans and a snug fitting black T-shirt. I walk in to find nobody else in the room, "When did the Supper Club hire a hot blonde dude?"

Danny turns and smiles directly at me in surprise, "Hey beautiful. I didn't think I'd get to see you today, Jacks. I thought you'd get here later and I have to go home tonight. Jackie time while her mom is at work." His hands are in his pockets, he's keeping his distance and trying to be work appropriate. I check the envelope Katy gave me and give Danny my extra room key.

"We all have things we have to do and it's going to be a busy weekend. I need to go unload, get settled in my room, and meet Katy for some girl time tonight."

Danny gives me a funny smirk, "Have you seen my office?"

"You have an office? I don't have an office."

Danny takes my hand and leads me to his office, "Let me show you my office." He closes the door behind us. "I don't think anybody else is here besides Katy, or I wouldn't chance being caught pulling you into my office. I don't want to mess this opportunity up." The next thing his lips do is press against mine while he holds my back to his office door. His hands go directly to my ass and he squeezes with his big strong hands. He stops and rests his forehead on mine, "I have to finish up a couple things for Katy and be home before 7:15pm, but know that I need you baby. It's been four days too long without you." Danny puts his arms around me and holds me while he claims me, completely. How his kiss can make me tingle down to my toes, I'll never understand. "I love you, baby. We'll find some time this weekend." He leads me out of his office and stops at one of the cooking areas. "Will you try this? I've been working on a couple recipes." Danny puts a small plate in front of me with a cookie on it that's been drizzled with chocolate in kind of a cross-hatch pattern, another that is two cookies sandwiched with a layer of chocolate filling, and a third that is a single cookie half coated in chocolate. There is also a sauce on the side.

"Have I ever turned down anything sweet?"

Danny laughs and feeds me a bite of the first cookie. It's a peanut butter cookie, that's very peanut buttery with dark chocolate drizzle and it's yummy. Then Danny gives me a bite of the sandwich cookie that's also peanut butter cookies and my eyes roll into the back of my head. Last, he feeds me a bite of the chocolate-coated peanut butter cookie and then another bite of it with the sauce, which seems to be some type of red wine reduction. "Okay, obviously the sandwich cookie was your favorite. What do you think about the other two?"

"Of course the sandwich cookie is my favorite, it has the most chocolate. I think all three are yummy, the first one is for someone that isn't as much of a chocolate fiend as I am. I'm not a fan of the sauce with the chocolate. If it's suppose to be like a play on peanut butter and jelly, maybe leave the chocolate out?"

Danny smiles, "I think it's a success because you got the peanut butter and jelly combo. I need to be catering to everybody's taste buds."

"Has Katy tried them?"

"No, she's busy."

"Katy is never too busy for food," and I take off with the dish heading directly into Katy's office. "Hey, I just sampled some new recipes and thought you should try them."

Katy turns and her eyes shine at the sight of food. She tries the first one and makes a yummy sound. She tries the second and nods her head. She tries the third, "What the hell is that? Chocolate doesn't belong on peanut butter and jelly." Danny standing behind and watching over my shoulder, rolls his eyes.

"Do you like the jelly sauce with the cookie without the chocolate? Which of the cookies do you like best?"

"Yes. The other two are equally yummy. What are you thinking?"

"Trio of Peanut Butter Cookies served with Milk Chocolate Ice Cream and Strawberry Sauce."

"Why didn't we put that on the menu?" Katy looks to Danny.

"I still have recipes that I'm working on. You have only tasted the recipes I feel are ready. I've been working on more, so we can update the menu at some point. Maybe switch out items that don't sell as well for new dishes. My creativity has been more focused on dessert lately." Danny gestures my direction. "Thank you for tasting, ladies." Danny picks up the plate and heads back to the kitchen. I follow him.

"I'm going to unload. Call me later if you can and I'll see you tomorrow, Danny." I blow him a kiss and switch gears. I get unloaded and into room 516 quickly. I freshen up a bit and hurry back to Katy.

I walk in on Katy having a meeting with the guys and she's irritated with them. She gives me a nod, "Guys, I have plans and didn't think you would show up after 6pm, so let's make it quick or pick it up in the morning."

"Cool, where are we going tonight?" Kyle stares at her anxiously like a dog getting ready to go for a walk on a leash.

"I don't know where you're going. I have some girl time planned," she stares at him decisively. "Here are all the notes and my suggestions on the menu and pricing, as well as an idea about selling CDs. Discuss it and get back to me with your decisions. Don't call me tonight." Katy stands up and grabs her purse, "Good night." She grabs me by the arm as she walks past and we don't stop until we're in the parking lot. "You have a vehicle?"

"Yep." I lead her to my truck and wait for further instructions.

"Manicure first, they close earlier." Katy plays navigator and we talk about what I want to shop for while we get our nails done, as well as where we're going to drink after shopping—Katy needs it. I get my nails done in a medium to dark red color called Snow White's Apple. Katy gets her nails done in black metallic called Constellation. She repeatedly tells me that I don't need to go shopping, George will take care of me. But, I finally get her to understand that I want an outfit that is how I think I should look for my set at the Supper Club, not necessarily George's take on what I wear everyday. I'm a jeans and T-shirt kind of girl and nothing is going to change that, but I'm not sure modern is my style for the Supper Club. I may need to be retro. Maybe I need to be a cross between Janis Joplin and modern singer/songwriter. I'm a throwback at heart. At the same time, this is Las Vegas where the glitz and glamour rules. I need boots, jeans, fringe, maybe a hat and vest or a jacket.

Katy pulls out her phone and dials, "George, what do you have for Jackie to wear opening night?" She stops and listens. "And shoes or boots?" She stops to listen again. "Like a moccasin? Uh huh, with a bell? Okay. What color? Right and what kind of style would you call that? And you've got all the accessories, anything with fringe?" Katy laughs, "Sounds good. You've got everybody handled, right?" Katy nods, "Just make them try the outfits on tomorrow, so you have time to make adjustments. Thanks." Katy hangs up on George and smiles at me, "I don't think you have anything to worry about, maybe we should find you some brown suede moccasin style boots or something like that with the fringe you want, probably shorter than your black suede boots. Otherwise, it sounds like he has you pegged and may have been playing dress-up with you last weekend. Let's go to the Minnetonka store to find you some boots and then go drink."

"Sounds like a plan. Should we go back to the Stardust to drink? We can make friends with a bartender. You can crash in my room tonight again if you want. The room has two beds this time."

Katy laughs, "I made sure it did after I found out you've been doing it with Danny, I don't want to sleep in your sex bed!"

I laugh with her and decide to play with her, "Yea, and man is it good sex. You wouldn't believe how…"

Katy cuts me off, "Please no. I don't want to hear it."

"So, what's the deal with Kyle? He was basically wrapped around you last weekend and you two were pretty friendly when we were out on the strip, but today you were ripping him a new one." I gaze at her wondering if she'll answer or ignore me.

"The guys are driving me up a wall this week. Let's find your boots, so we can go drink." Interesting, answering and ignoring at the same time, now that's skill.

We get back to the Stardust, no luck on the boots, and find a bar. Katy gets plastered on shots of Goldschlager and I relax with a few Midori and Sprites. She reads me the riot act for being a light weight, but I let it go and don't explain it's my missing Danny drink. We manage to get to my room in one piece and pass out.

CHAPTER NINETEEN

I don't need to be at the club until noon on Friday, but I have work to do. I get up with Katy, make my sales calls, and manage to pop in for surprise visits with three of my regular customers.

I walk into the Supper Club at 11:30am with enough time to check in with Katy, wave at the chef working with his new staff, and try my opening night wardrobe. I need to trust people more, George has my outfit perfect: black suede flat bottom boots that are about mid-calf high, blue jeans with embroidered flower detailing in red on the front of the legs, short black suede vest with long fringe and a fitted red lace see-through camisole with a band running below my breasts that the neckline drops to with a nude foundation built into it. George has a pair of round hippie glasses, at least two-dozen bangle bracelets in varying metals and materials, 2 extra large red bandanas, a red feather boa, and a box of rings and other jewelry in my accessory bin. Today, I'm me in jeans and a classic rock T-shirt with my suede boots, no make-up and my hair is tied up in a knot. I take the hippie glasses with me, get Robyn to cut the bottom off of the T-shirt I'm wearing and use one of the bandanas as a belt. Nobody says a word. Today is all about business and I think the vocalists need a good idea of who I am. I walk back through the kitchen wanting approval from my hard rock man.

Danny examines me from head to toe, taking plenty of time at my hips and breasts, "Jackie, can I talk to you in my office real quick. I want to get your feedback on the tasting you did for me last night." I walk to his office and he follows me in, closing the door behind us. "Are you fucking trying to kill me? You're so fucking hot! It's like you saw my dreams and know how I see you." I smile at him dirtily and don't speak. I simply touch his chest and drag my finger down until it reaches his jeans. Unbutton his fly quickly as I drop to my knees and stroke him with both hands while I suck and lick at his tip.

Over the loud speaker I hear Katy, "Ladies and gentlemen, its that time. Guys and Jackie, please meet me at the table. Performers be ready for your turn and prepared for instant feedback. This needs to be perfect Ladies!"

I stare into Danny's eyes and lick him from base to tip, "Sorry, I don't know what I was thinking. I shouldn't have started without being able to finish. But, you taste as good as your food."

"Don't worry, babe. We'll get a little time before I have to go home tonight." I stand up and he kisses me on the forehead, "Love you, Jacks." I get out of his office quickly and shut the door behind me to allow him time to adjust. I notice my boots are dusty from the floor and dust them off quickly before anybody notices and catches on. Not the smartest thing I've done.

I grab a Dr. Pepper from the refrigerator and get to the table before Katy and the guys.

There's a schedule sitting on the table:

```
Supper Club Set Schedule
Saturday Set One - Jackie
Saturday Set Two - Jackie
Sunday -
Monday Dark
Tuesday Dark
Wednesday -
Thursday -
Friday Set One -
Friday Set Two -
```

Katy sits down next to me and I'm curious, "Katy, nobody else is penciled in for any of the sets for the week. Where is the complete schedule?"

"There isn't one. These ladies don't know which nights they'll be performing and it can change every week." Katy gives me the run down.

"What about the girls that are singing tomorrow night?" Thinking they must know.

"About that, you're picking who sings when based on the run-through today. They're already aware and that should help them do their best today."

I stare at Katy in shock.

"It's not a big deal! Just do it. Make the show great." She smiles at me and I can almost hear her telepathically 'pull up your big girl panties.'

"How many singers per set?"

"Four, forty-five minute sets per show, including you."

"Can all of the vocalists sing opening night? Maybe what they're competing for today is how many songs? I think it will help to have everyone here opening night." Katy relays the idea to the guys and we both wait for a response.

The guys look at each other and make a couple of faces. They're so weird. Then Kyle nods in agreement with something communicated silently and turns to Katy, "We like it, but we want Jackie to perform her full set at both opening night shows. She's our Music Director and we want to showcase her as the headlining singer. Why not make opening night the best we have to offer? Makes sense."

Katy stands up and yells out, "Singers, please line up on stage together. For opening night, everyone will get to sing. You're not singing for your set today. You're singing for which song or songs you'll be asked to perform for opening night. Our Music Director, Jackie, will be judging you today and making those decisions. You'll know the results before you leave today. Now, let's get rolling! Thank you, ladies."

I open my folder of set lists and make fresh notes as they go, scoring each song and each vocalist. Some of the songs are must haves. A few of the vocalists have stepped up, including a couple of them that I gave songs to that had never heard the song before. I'm last to take my turn on stage and run through my set list. I call an audible with Archie, changing my Janis song to "Piece of My Heart" because, well it's how it needs to be. At the end of my set, I turn to the band and thank them for their hard work.

"Jackie, pick a song near the end of your set that has some opportunities for instrumental solos and introduce the members of the band," Katy calls out. I turn to the band and though I love them all, I only know Archie's name.

"Okay. Archie, are you guys going to be around awhile tonight? I need to finalize the set list for opening night and then maybe we can practice band introduction? Can you decide on which song you want to use?"

"Sure thing. We need the set list when you're done, so we aren't going anywhere." Archie and the band discuss the songs on my set list as I go sit at the table and review my notes.

I highlight each vocalist's best song and add up the time, so I know how much time I have left to play with. I add in any remaining songs I've categorized as must haves and make sure each vocalist has at least two songs, then I go through my list based strictly on my scoring and choose the highest scoring offerings until I run out of set time. "Katy, you want to double check me on the timing?" I hand her the list. "Ladies, I'm going to call out the songs you will be performing tomorrow night and the final order will be posted backstage when you arrive tomorrow. Archie, please let me know if you have any concerns." Katy gives me an approving nod and I read out the list. I get mixed reactions from the vocalists, but I expected that. Archie gives me a thumbs up. "Katy, I'll get you a list in order before I leave tonight."

Katy and the guys go back to whatever they do, while I go work out the band introductions and chat with Archie about the opening night set list. I put the songs and singers in order while the band runs through what they think their solos will be. I memorize the names of the band members and hope I remember them tomorrow. Then I walk into Katy's office with the set list for opening night.

"Thank you. I need you to set the schedule for the rest of the week, too. Only four per show," and she hands me the schedule I was reviewing earlier. I gave the vocalists with more songs opening night, more shows per week, and the vocalist that scored highest for me gets to sing last. No brainer. I hand it back to Katy in less than ten minutes. She's stunned, "Thank you."

"I told you not to be surprised." I smile at her, "What else would you like me to do today?"

"Take your man back to your room and order room service for dinner. You both need to relax and get to bed early. He's going to want to pick up his food order at 6am. Don't make him be in charge of the food tonight," Katy means it.

"I'll do my best. I don't know if he has to go home tonight."

CHAPTER TWENTY

I walk into the kitchen and find Danny alone, writing the schedule for food prep on a big white board, and assigning prep to his staff. "Hey babe, do you have any plans tonight?" I ask in my sexy voice.

Danny's irritated, "I was planning on spending a couple of hours with you and then checking in at home and not going home tonight. But, she hasn't gotten home from work and she should've been home three hours ago."

"So, you have to go home now," the sadness in my voice takes over, even though I understand.

"Yes. I need to get to bed early tonight anyway. If I can get away, I'll come back when she gets home." Danny smiles at me, neither of us happy with the situation. "I'll check in on you in the morning, Jacks."

I can't believe how upset I am right now. I really hate her. She's doing this to keep him from being with anyone else and she doesn't even know it's me. Pretty childish to play the 'if I can't have you, they can't have you' game. Imagine what she'd do if she found out about us. She must hate that he's happy.

She must know he's found someone to date that makes him happy again. She must know he's getting laid. Yeah, I really hate her. I bet it's tearing her up that she can't keep him for herself. Danny doesn't deserve this, he deserves to be happy and we should be able to be together without hiding it.

"You know where to find me. Only us, Danny. I'll always wait for you." I turn to head out of the Supper Club.

"Babe!" Danny calls after me and I spin around to focus on him. "I really wanted to be with you tonight. I know this is kind of silly, but I've been carrying the cork from our champagne last weekend in my pocket and I twisted the cage into a ring for you. I know it's corny." Danny hands me the twisted metal with a shiny silver cap that has a fleur de lis design pressed into it. "You don't have to wear it. I want you to have it."

I give it back to him and hold both of my hands out, "Put it on me." I gaze into his eyes and watch which finger he chooses to put it on.

"I love you, Jacks. I want this to be more. Someday this will be a real ring, maybe this can be a placeholder. A promise." Danny slides the champagne cage fashioned into a ring onto my left ring finger. The cap is big, but I love it.

My heart is happy. I gaze into Danny's eyes happier than I've ever been, "I love you, too, Danny." I reach up and kiss him before I head up to my room for the night.

———

My room feels empty and my brain won't stop pulling me into a million different directions. I make busy work for myself and call my friends that are coming to opening night. I run through the band members like a game of memory, matching their name with the instrument they play. I don't have to worry about what I'm wearing tomorrow or my make-up or my hair, George and Marni will take care of me. My songs run through me naturally, requiring no effort to remember the lyrics and it's the right choice to have all of the vocalists sing opening night. I wish Danny was here. We'll get our time tomorrow and his food will be yummy. I need to relax.

I take a long shower and enjoy the hot water beating down on me. It relaxes me and I listen to the sound of the drops as they spray around me like rain. Finally getting the voices to stop yelling in my head, I close my eyes and I'm flooded with memories. Danny walking up to the no-tell motel with dinner and finding me locked out with no shoes. Danny saying sweet things the night we met, asking if I was his angel. Tasting his lips as I remember the first signs of falling, making out in the photo booth. His voice asking me, 'Are you mine?' when he claimed me in the parking lot at this very casino. Danny protecting me and taking care of me. When he isn't with me he's always watching out for me. Suffering without me so I'd move on with my life. Danny wanted me happy when his only choice was to be miserable. His hands on me, knowing how to make me happy, knowing how to drive me crazy, knowing how to make me scream his name. I vividly recall the first time I couldn't control myself around him and took him bare, right in the front seat of my truck. Our phone calls playing in my head. The pain of my torment from keeping my lie when I shouldn't have. His face that horrible day he told me about his indiscretion, that turned into his confession of love and good-bye. The one thing that rings through to me over and over, in between every memory and right in the middle of some, is the tone of his voice when he calls me Jacks. Sweet, sincere, and unwavering heartfelt emotion all conveyed in the pet name he gave me. The first weekend we spent together, yep, that's when I became his Jacks.

I turn off the shower and step out of the steam, drying off and tying my hair up into a knot. I pull on the threadbare Ramone's T-shirt and my favorite sweatpants, grab the remote and curl up in bed to watch a movie.

CHAPTER TWENTY-ONE

At 6am I'm startled by the phone ringing. Today is the big day, opening night of the Supper Club. What the hell? Why is somebody calling me at 6am? Without opening my eyes, "It's 6am."

"Yea, good morning, Jacks." Danny doesn't sound like the happy-go-lucky Danny I've been spending more and more time with.

"Hey, babe. Are you coming to visit me this morning?" I ask sleepily.

"I'm sorry about this. I don't know what else to do," He's worked up in a way that I've never heard until now. "She didn't come home. I don't have a babysitter for during the day today. Her Uncle Tony is at work until 10am. I need to get the food order for the Supper Club and I can't take her with me. Jackie's still sleeping, and usually sleeps until around 8am. Can I bring her to your room and let her sleep there while I get the food for the club?" Danny sighs, "I know it's a lot to ask."

Okay, I'm awake. I quickly process the information that's been thrown at me. "Sure. Whatever you need. It's a team effort to get what we want, right?" The words come out of my mouth and I mean them, even though I've never babysat in my life, and I'd like to sleep another few hours.

"You're awesome, babe. Go back to sleep, I'll knock when we get there. I promise to make this up to you." Danny hangs up and I fall back to sleep like nothing happened and I'm not going to be babysitting a small child at any moment.

Theres knocking on my door and I jump out of bed. I open the door thinking Danny will have his hands full, carrying a sleeping Jackie. But, I'm greeted by Jackie herself standing there and grinning from ear to ear. "Good morning. Daddy said I can take you to breakfast, but we can't have ice cream. Did I wake you up?"

"Hi Jackie! How will he know if we have ice cream?" I make funny eyes at the little girl.

Jackie glances at the wall next to her, "Daddy heard you." She claps her hands against the sides of her legs and walks into my room like she owns the place.

Danny looks into the room and shakes his head at his little girl, "She woke up while I was getting ready. Going to breakfast will give you something to do and make it easy on you. Tony will come by and say hi, he's on walkie 4 if you need him. I'll meet you at the coffee shop in less than an hour. Thank you, Jacks." Danny squeezes my hand. "Jackie, have fun at breakfast with Jacks, okay?"

"Yes, Daddy. I'm okay." Jackie waves the cutest little girl wave ever at Danny and turns away from him.

Danny rolls his eyes, and stares at me still wearing the old T-shirt. He motions that he wants to reach out and touch me, but knows better. "I know, go take care of business," I give him permission to leave me and Jackie.

I secure the door and turn to Jackie, "Let me change real quick and we'll go get breakfast, okay?"

"Okay." Jackie watches me, every move.

I change into my jeans and my Bon Jovi T-shirt, and pull on my boots. I let my hair down and quickly brush it out. I gather up keys, money, and my phone, loading my pockets. On a whim, I grab the hippie glasses off the dresser and slide them up on my head to hold my hair back. I turn to Jackie, "Shall we?" She smiles at me and grabs my hand as we leave the room and walk through the hotel to the coffee shop. The hostess seats us in a booth and leaves us menus, a breakfast menu for me and a kid's menu with crayons for Jackie. All of a sudden I'm hungry and my stomach is growling. "What would you like for breakfast?" I ask Jackie.

"Maybe pancakes or waffles. Bacon."

"Do you like strawberries?" Jackie nods her head. "They make a waffle with whipped cream and strawberries on it. It's not ice cream, but it's close. What do you think?"

"Yes! Daddy didn't say no whipped cream." Her eyes shine happily.

The waitress takes our order and brings me coffee, Jackie hot cocoa. We sip while we wait for our breakfast. Jackie looks around at everything curiously. Her brain is working at a million miles a minute and has questions that she's not asking. "Have you been here before?" I ask her.

"Yes, Daddy works here. He told me he works in a different part now and that he gets to cook. Is he cooking breakfast?"

"He's the chef over at the Supper Club. He doesn't cook here at the coffee shop. Your Daddy is a very good cook."

"Daddy is the best cook." Her love for him loyal and evident.

Tony walks up and sits in the booth next to Jackie, "Hey there, Sunshine," and she gives him a big hug.

"Hi, Uncle Tony," Jackie is loud and gives him a big toothy smile.

The waitress brings him some coffee. Tony and Jackie

interact like family, she's happy to have him near and laughs at
him while he plays with her.

Tony focuses his attention on me, "Are you doing okay
with this?"

"We're doing fine. Just two girls out having breakfast
together." I smile at Tony and Jackie copies me.

"Okay then, I'll leave you two beautiful ladies to your
breakfast and see you both soon." Tony leaves the table and
takes his coffee with him.

The waitress brings our food, we both have a waffle with
whipped cream and strawberries. Plus, we share a plate of
bacon. Jackie's eyes light up at the bacon and she gets whipped
cream on her nose. Danny walks up and steals a piece of the
bacon as he slides into the booth next to Jackie. "Hey my
angel, are you enjoying your breakfast?" He gazes at me and
smiles as Jackie nods her head.

"Jacks said we could have whipped cream, it's okay
because it's not ice cream."

"It makes sense to me," Danny swipes some whipped
cream with one of the strawberries and sucks it off before
biting into the berry. "I need to go to my office and make a
call. Why don't you finish your breakfast and come find me?"
He turns to me for approval and I nod. He takes off for the
Supper Club and we finish our breakfast quietly, both of us
eating happily.

When we finish, I charge breakfast to my room and grab
Jackie's hand for the walk across the casino. "This is cool, you
get to see our work."

Jackie turns to me questioning, "You work with my
Daddy?"

"We work at the same place, but we do different things.
Your Daddy is in charge of the kitchen and I'm in charge of the
music. I get to sing while people eat your Daddy's food."

"Cool." She says copying me.

We walk into the Supper Club and Katy is in her office, so I stop, "Good morning. This is my friend Jackie."

Katy glares at me questioningly, "Nice to meet you, Jackie. I'm Katy. What brings you here so early this morning?"

The sweet girl gives Katy a big smile, burps, and giggles, "Daddy needed to work, so me and Jacks had breakfast. Daddy works here. I want to see where he works."

"We're stopping to say hi on our way to the kitchen. Everything is handled. Call me if you need me for anything," and we walk to the kitchen to find Danny on the phone in his office. We walk around the kitchen investigating everything, all the clean and shiny stainless steel, the hanging utensils and the cases full of food. My phone rings and the call is coming from inside the kitchen. "Hello?"

"Jacks, she still didn't get home. It's a huge day for me and…" I cut him off.

"Give her a tour of your kitchen. She wants to see where you work now. Let me talk to Katy a minute and try to work something out. We only need until 10am, right?"

"Yes. Okay," Danny hangs up and comes out of his office. He picks up Jackie and swings her around, leaving her sitting on his shoulder. He carries her around the kitchen showing her everything and telling her about it.

I go back to Katy, "So, anyway, her mom never came home from work yesterday and still hasn't. She was the babysitter today. He has a babysitter for later this afternoon and her Uncle will take her when he gets off work at 10am. Her Uncle is Tony from Stardust Security."

"With the afro?" Katy gawks at me confused.

"Yes. Danny wants to start cooking early, first night as chef and all. I'm not supposed to be here yet, but would you mind if Jackie and I hang out at the piano?" Maybe I can show her some music or something to keep her entertained.

"No problem. I doubt anybody else will show up before 10am."

"Thank you." I go back to the kitchen and catch the tail end of the tour. "Jackie, would you like to see what I do?"

Danny and Jackie glance at each other, she nods her head excitedly. I reach my hand out and she comes running over to me. "I'll be back, Daddy." I gaze at him as his heart melts. He didn't count on his little girl running away from him to hang out with his... interesting, what am I? Girlfriend? His woman? Lover? Partner? Soulmate? We don't have an appropriate classification. He didn't count on Jackie running off to play with me.

We go backstage and walk out to the mic at center stage. I show her what I do and sing a song for her, then we go over to the piano where we talk about different instruments and I ask if she's ever seen a piano before. I play part of a song for her and her eyes get big. I play the piano part from "Home Sweet Home" by Motley Crue and she recognizes it, so I show her how to play it. Tony comes walking up and stops to observe. He holds a finger up at me, leaves, and is back in less than two minutes with Danny, both of them staying out of Jackie's sight and watching the little girl take on the grand piano with Motley Crue. The happiness shines on her face as she makes music confidently like an old pro, even though she can't reach the ground or the pedals for that matter. Jackie plays it a few more times, then stops and claps giddily, happy with herself.

Tony claps from the audience, "Great job, Sunshine!" Jackie blushes. "How about hanging out with me today?"

Jackie turns and gazes up at me, she wants to play more. "We can play more next time. I have to get to work, too. I'll show you another song next time. How does that sound?" Jackie nods excitedly and walks to Tony at the edge of the stage. He lifts her to the floor and she waves at me as they go to check in with Danny before they leave.

CHAPTER TWENTY-TWO

I walk to Katy's office and lean in her doorway, "I'm here early, so what can I do to help?"

"Are you playing the part of problem solver today?" Katy is in full on smart-ass mode.

"Apparently, though I don't remember auditioning for the role. I can go back to bed and leave you alone, or I can help you with whatever needs to be done."

"I have a job that would be perfect for you. Can you check with the chef and confirm that he has everything he needs for tonight's service? Take this to him, so he can see what the final menu looks like. And, find out if we're running any specials tonight. It's going to be a long day for him, maybe have him look at his schedule and find a time he can take a break for a nap, food, something." Katy's serious, but I love the idea of 'something.'

"Chef!" I call out to get his attention. "I'm helping Katy with some things this morning since I'm here early and she put me on her chef tasks." I smile at him as he walks toward me.

"Yes, ma'am. Anything for you." Danny gazes at me with a dirty glint in his eye.

"This is for Katy, what I want is a whole different thing." I lock my eyes with his, full of intent. "Business first. Here is the final menu. Katy wanted you to have a copy of it. Do you have everything you need for tonight's service? Are we running any specials tonight?"

Danny is happy to have the final printed product, his menu. "I have everything I need for tonight, probably extra. I ordered enough for two nights, since I don't know what the diners will order. I've been thinking about a special." A deep fryer beeps and he walks across the kitchen to pull something fried out, tossing it with a mix of things and dumping a pile on the plate. He brings the plate to me and it's hand cut French fries. "Try these with this sauce."

The French fries are perfectly crisp on the outside, not greasy at all and they have a mix of salt, black pepper and something else on them, something nutty and cheesy. Then I dip in the sauce, yum, yum, yum! It's a barbecue sauce with a hint of whiskey. "Yum! Tell me what it is."

Danny gets a confident stance of victory, "Pommes Frites, which are basically twice fried fries, tossed with salt, pepper, and Parmesan. The sauce is a whiskey barbecue sauce with a touch of heat at the end. Did you get the heat?"

I got the heat as he was talking and it was a perfect finish. "Yea, nice ending." I turn to leave, taking the plate with me and Danny follows after me as I walk into Katy's office. "Katy, more food to try." Katy tries a fry, then another with the sauce.

"What's this?" Katy stares at Danny.

"Do you like it?" He wants her opinion.

"Yes, best fries I've ever had and that sauce is what adults want instead of ketchup."

"I'd like to start everyone with a sample of it tonight, a thank you for joining us on our opening night. Nothing big, a small dish of sauce and maybe a dozen fries." Danny waits for permission.

"What's it called?"

"Twice Fried Taters with Jacks Sauce. It's Pommes frites, but I think that's too formal for the Supper Club."

"Jacks Sauce?" Katy eyeballs him.

"It has Jack Daniels in it and I created it with my Jacks in mind. Sweet, smoky, and with a kick."

"What's the cost?" Katy is all business today.

Danny stops and thinks, "Less than $1 per person."

"Can you get it down to $.60 per person?"

"Sure, can I serve it per party instead of per person? Full tables get a big plate, couples get a smaller serving, etc."

"I like it. Do it. Make sure you have plenty of the Brownies to Make Blondie Love You, those are going to go like crazy tonight and I want at least one left over for me."

"Yes, ma'am," Danny is pleased with himself and Katy kicks us out of her office, keeping the fries and sauce.

Back in the kitchen, "So, you have everything you need for tonight. No special because you're giving them the fries and sauce?" I want to make sure I've got my task from Katy handled.

"Yea. I don't want to throw the kitchen off on opening night. But, I don't have everything I need." Danny pulls me close and whispers in my ear, "I need you, Jacks. Some serious alone time. Right now I would take any time alone with you. I want to feel your lips, taste you... touch you."

His breath at my ear sends me off track and I recover quickly as I remember that the last piece of business might get us alone. "Katy wants you to take a break sometime today. It's going to be a long day and you need to be fresh at service. At what point today can you get out of the kitchen for a bit to take a nap or eat or just take a break and clear your head?"

"I need to be here all day. It's opening night."

"Katy disagrees and she's in charge. Check your prep schedule. Is there one hour where you can be out of the kitchen at any time today?" I add under my breath, "Preferably before 2pm, so I can spend the time with you."

Danny smiles, "I've got everything that needs a long cook in already and my staff will handle most of the prep when they get here. I need to add the taters and sauce to the board, and being the important day it is, I think I should be here the whole time my staff is here. How about I break in fifteen minutes?"

"Sounds good. I need to get back to Katy. You want to meet me at the room?" I make sexy eyes at him and shake my ass as I'm walking away.

Danny makes a deep male groan, "Yes."

I go to Katy and fill her in on all things kitchen. I advise her that he's going to take a break before his staff gets there and has things in cooking. I fake yawn, "So if you don't need me for the next hour or so, I'm going to go nap in my room."

"Sure you are. Good, go have fun. I want you both relaxed tonight. It will get us the best results. No grumpy chef and a satisfied music director. Get out!" Katy pushes me out of her office.

CHAPTER TWENTY-THREE

I go back to my room and take my boots off. I turn on the hard rock station, trade my jeans for my sweats and my Bon Jovi T-shirt for the old Ramones shirt. I kick back on the bed, propping my head up on the pillow and relax.

Danny crawls into bed next to me and I don't even hear the door. He pulls the blankets up over us, "Jacks, lets hide from the world for awhile." He kisses me gently and holds me possessively. Running his tongue across my lips, I open for him and he rolls me underneath him as he takes control of me, trying to satisfy both of our needs. His need is out of control and he slides his hand into my sweatpants, finding my wet heat. His body reacts and he slides a finger in, "I want you so bad, Jacks."

"Take me, Danny. Please." He slides in a second finger, working me and driving me wild. "Danny!" I call out as I writhe at his touch. He wants me. I grind against him and take control of the kiss, aggressively sucking at his tongue and holding his face. He pulls my pants off and he's between my legs. His hard length rubbing on me and wanting in, but something is stopping him. I reach for his cock and stroke him lightly a few times before I slide his tip inside me, pushing my body against him until I have him buried deep. Danny is silent and strong, but his body gives him away. He moves slowly, pushing deliciously deeper and breathing raggedly. He touches my sensitive nub, circling it slowly and closing in on it with more pressure. I scream out his name and buck wildly without warning, experiencing how hard he is as I go off around him. Danny slams into me repeatedly. Pounding me hard, needing to get off with me tight around him, moving faster and faster, the hot friction between us sets me off again. My body needing more of him. I move with him and he gets harder. His whole body tenses at his release and he holds me tight against him. I feel his heat, his blood rushing through him and his heart pounding wildly. Our heat is crazy and we've been apart for only about a week. My body is ringing with joy, Danny and my music is all I want.

Danny rolls to his side and pulls me back to him, spooning me and holding my hand. He touches my hands, every individual finger, every knuckle, and my soft palms. "Jacks, you're still wearing the champagne cage."

"You put it on me and I'm never taking it off," I say softly and my heart glows with warmth.

"I wouldn't have made it today without you. You fix everything, Jacks." Danny's in line with my problem solver title today. "I need you and seeing you with Jackie makes..., I can't explain what it does to me. Not to mention that my little girl can play Motley Crue."

"I thought you'd like it if she played something hard rock. It gave us something to do and it seemed like she likes music." I was hesitant. I didn't asked Danny first or anything, but what do you expect from a problem solver?

"It was perfect. You're perfect." Danny kisses the back of my neck and glides his hand over me, smoothing over my skin like silk.

"I told her I would teach her another song next time. We need to get her a keyboard."

"Okay, after we take a nap." Danny's fading and I set an alarm. We both need to relax for the night ahead and we don't have much time.

I wake up before the alarm goes off and sit up straight, hit with the reality of tonight. I'm headlining the show I'm Music Director for and we open tonight. We open in a few hours. In a matter of minutes really. This is the first time I'll be performing a full set that's not for practice. Every emotion in existence hits me at the same time. I jump out of bed and start wandering the room aimlessly, tinkering with the radio, lining my shoes up neatly, tossing trash in the wastebasket, not having a clue what to do, and needing to do something. "Jacks? What are you doing?" Danny is lying on his side with his head supported by his hand, watching me closely.

"Did you know I'm headlining tonight? Performing my whole set at the end of each seating tonight? The other vocalists are all singing tonight and only a few songs each, because the Music Director had the wonderful idea that everyone should get to sing on opening night and the guys want the Music Director to sing her whole set. I'm the Music Director. I did this to myself. If the music choice sucks, its all me! I've never performed a full set for an audience. I've only done it in practice. Oh, my boss has two whole tables tonight and invited my co-workers from the warehouse. Dot is supposed to be here. I have no idea who else will show up." I shut up when I notice I'm breathing erratically and freaking the fuck out, worse I'm doing it in front of Danny.

"I get it, babe. It's a big night for us. I feel the make it or break it pressure. I made it through this morning and you made that happen. Honestly, you don't even need luck. Jacks, you were meant to do this. You belong on stage. Your voice, the way you feel music—people will love it and I may be the only person that knows why. It's because you do everything with your whole heart and you mean it completely. It all comes out in your music, Jacks. Just like I never wondered why you didn't tell me you love me before, you didn't need to because you showed me every second I was with you and you still do. My biggest worry should be how I'm going to keep you when everybody else gets to see who you are. You're going to put your heart out on the Supper Club stage tonight and everyone in the audience is going to want a piece of it."

There it was, the reason I needed to go back to "Piece of My Heart" by Janis Joplin. I didn't even know why, but my Danny does. "Thank you, Danny. No matter what, my heart only belongs to you." I move to the bed and bend over to give him a kiss.

Danny gazes into the mirror behind me, "Are you being a tease?" He moves quickly and grabs me by the waist, "Let me see here..." turning me around and pulling me back to sit on his lap at the edge of the bed. "No, that's not what I want." He lifts me up and brings me back down, this time onto Tiger. Filling me instantly and making me forget everything else that's happening today. "Oh yeah, that's much better. Don't you think, Jacks?" His hot breath at my ear from behind me. He reaches around in front of me and touches our connection, gliding his fingers across my dripping wet folds. "You're so wet, Jacks. You feel so good on me, wrapped around my dick like this." He has one arm wrapped around my body below my breasts holding me to him, and the other still touching my sex while he continues to whisper, "You make me so hard, I can't help myself when I'm near you." He kisses my neck open mouthed, moving toward my ear. I grind against him, unable to do anything else from the position he's holding me in and he pinches my clit between two of his fingers causing me to cry out. "Are you a bad girl, Jacks? Bad girls tease and grind on hard cocks, especially when huge cocks like mine are shoved up into them. Bad girls want more than that. Bad girls want to get fucked, they want to get bent over or folded in half and fucked until they can't stand. Bad girls like to get fucked until they're brainless. You feel my hard dick shoved up into you, Jacks? Tell me what it makes you want."

My voice is shaky, "I want you to bend me over and take me from behind, hard."

"I can make that happen, but first I have other business to tend to." He pinches my clit again and strokes it between his two fingers, rubbing it hard and fast, setting me on fire until I scream. He pushes up into me somehow giving me more of him and putting more pressure on my sensitive nub, knowing exactly how to send me over the edge uncontrollably. "Fuck, Jacks you feel so good when you do this. But, you're a bad girl and you need to be bent over." Danny stands up, lifting me with him and starts to slide out of me. He turns me toward the bed and leans over until I'm on all fours. Then pushes all the way into me, over and over. He stands up straight, spreading my knees on the bed and slams into me harder with his deeper access.

"Danny! Oh, fuck me." I hear myself screaming and calling out his name as if I'm listening from the room next door. Danny continues to slam into me, pounding hard in and out, in and out, in and out, and I can hardly stay up on my hands and knees.

"That's right, my bad girl. I know this is what bad girls like." He pushes into me hard and holds himself in deep, pushing against me. I'm stretched as far as I can go and extremely full, maxed out. He reaches for my sensitive nub, "It's time to explode for me, baby," and presses the magic button, I have maximum detonation almost instantly. Danny slams into me a few more times, "Fuck, Jacks. How do you do this to me every fucking time? I just want to…" he growls some incoherent noises and I feel him come hard. We both collapse on the bed in a heap, unable to breathe at the same time that my alarm goes off. I lie there for a few minutes and let the alarm go off, fuck it.

"It's time to take over the world, Danny. Let's do this!" He pulls me to him, kissing me and giving us the strength we need.

"I love you, Jacks. Go rock that place." He leans his forehead to mine as we regain control.

"I love you, Danny. Go show Vegas their hottest new chef."

We get dressed quickly and go back to the Supper Club together, without caring what everybody thinks. It's time to be strong and show them what we've got.

CHAPTER TWENTY-FOUR

I walk to the kitchen with Danny like we're in high school and we have to part to go to different classrooms. He gives me a quick kiss, "You got this, babe. I'll be listening. I'll save you some dinner and dessert."

I report in with Katy, "Your chef has taken a break and will be fresh for the night. I've delivered him back to the kitchen. I'm going to get in the mood on stage, then visit with George and Marni before the other performers get here. Okay?"

"Sounds like just what the doctor ordered. Some of us around here could really use something to change our mood, get us motivated for opening night and out of our heads. It sounds like you have already managed to do that." Katy glares at me and shakes her head.

"How are you doing, Katy? Is there something else I can do to help you?" I don't want her freaking out tonight, or maybe we need to lock the guys in a closet or something.

"No, I think some music will do it. That's what I need. Rock it loud and proud, Jackie. Have you considered using Jacks as your stage name?" Katy stares at me waiting for a response.

"I've never considered using a stage name. One of the bands I sang back up for in Hollywood always introduced me to the crowd as 'Kitten,' but that was them having fun with me."

Katy shakes her head, "What about Jacks?"

"Danny is the only one who calls me Jacks."

"Do you like it?" Katy is digging at me.

"I love it when he calls me Jacks. Might be something about his tone when he says it, I don't know." Now I'm distracted and thinking about Danny.

"Focus! I think the audience will respond to Jacks better than Jackie. I think that you have a slight stage persona and using Jacks on stage will help you develop that."

In my perfect British accent, "Should I use my British accent, too? I did that routine for longer than I should've and I'm very good at it. Sounds great when I'm singing Handel's Messiah." I push my luck being a smart-ass with Katy.

She stares at me blankly, "Really? All that? Stage name or no stage name?"

"Katy, do you think that Jacks is something more private between me and Danny? I don't want to be making fun of it." I finally spill the truth.

Katy takes a deep breath, "I never know where you're going until you finally put it out there. You crazy girl. I think using the name he gave you is a good thing, it shows how much it means to you and that you want to share that with the world. You think about him when you're performing, right?"

"Yea. Not the whole time, but certain lyrics take me to him." It's like giving away my life story, but she's already read it.

"I think you should be Jacks." Katy says with certainty.

"You know best. Let's do it." Jacks does kind of sound like a rocker. I'm a rocker. "Then I'm going to the stage, and listen for me because I'll be talking, not just singing." I give Katy a hug. "Thanks for everything, I need help with this stuff."

I walk out on stage and greet the band. They all seem to be in the right state of mind. "Archie, you and the band in the mood to rock it for a few? We need to get this place pumped up and moving for opening night."

"You ready to bring it?" Archie taunts me.

"I'm thinking, 'Piece of My Heart,' Aerosmith, and whatever you want to throw at me. Keep it rockin'. Uh, I want to talk a little and I need to practice running through band introduction. Does that work?" I get a nod. I take the mic, "Hey everybody, welcome to the Supper Club. Thanks to the band for indulging me in some rock before show time. Katy, I hope this is what you were hoping for. My love, I know you can hear me—this is for you. By the way, I'm Jacks and this is my stage debut. 1 2 3 4!" Archie gives me an approving grin and starts in on the guitar intro to "Piece of My Heart." I'm somehow empowered and the song flows through me, part of me. I feel like a superhero, unstoppable. At the end of the song I'm on a high and yell out "Wooooo!" I turn to the mic, "Okay, the band is calling the rest of the songs. I've requested an Aerosmith tune next, but who knows what we'll get." Then the band starts in with driving guitar and drums on Aerosmith's "Love in An Elevator." I can't believe it, I toss my head back, untie my hair to let it fall loose around me, and I'm free of inhibitions like never before as I make the song my own. It's exhilarating as it comes to an end and I take the mic, "That brings back some memories." The band and I keep going for the better part of an hour. Approving sounds come from Katy's office, as well as some, "You rock, Jacks!" from the kitchen.

I make my way to wardrobe and greet the team, my high from the stage still following me around. "I'm here to be first and ready before the others get here. Are you ready for me?"

"George first," Marni examines my hair. "What did you do to your hair?"

"Nothing. It's been on top of my head in a knot, until I pulled it down while I was singing." I stare at her wondering why and waiting to find out what I did wrong.

"Hmm, I like it. It's got some wave, but still kind of long and straight. Go see George. George! Your first victim is here."

I shake my head as I walk back to George. George smiles at me, "I've been waiting for you," and hands me a hanger with my wardrobe for the night. "Put it on. I want to make sure you're perfect. Tonight, you're my star." I change into the blue jeans with the red embroidered outline of flowers and the red camisole. I gaze at my reflection in the mirror and I'd be happy to go out on stage just like this. I pull on the black suede boots that George has set out for me and they fit perfectly, like everything else. I step out of the changing room with the fringed vest in my hand and turn to George. "Yea, you're right, you don't need the vest. Start with it and hang it over the stool they'll have out there for you if you feel like taking it off." George checks every detail of my outfit. I imagine accessories flying through his head, while he digs into my accessory bin. "Let's put together your accessories without the vest, then see if it's too much when you have the vest on." He gets all of the bangle bracelets, all the metal on one wrist and other materials on the other. "The feather boa might be a bit much, maybe a prop you can tie around the mic stand. If you go without the vest, a bandana might be nice around your neck or as a head-band, or we can tie the two bandanas together to use as a belt or even replace your camisole with the bandanas, what do you think?"

"I'm intrigued by the bandana top idea, but not willing to go there on opening night. I'll be afraid it's going to fall off or something."

"Fair enough, wardrobe malfunction is a thing. I'll have the girls make a couple different bandana tops for you to try and maybe wear next weekend."

"Not a headband, the belt or neckerchief would both be fine. Do your magic, George." George ties the two bandanas together and loops them through the belt loops on my jeans, tying the ends into a rabbit ears style of knot and manipulating the ends until they're perfect.

"No hippie glasses on stage, those were because I knew you would love them. Let's find you a couple of rings and something for around your neck." George pulls out a wide silver band and makes it a thumb ring, then a ring of clear and red crystals that he slides on my middle finger, both on my right hand. He moves to my left hand, "Huh, the ring you're wearing works. Where'd you get that? I like it. It's kind of vintage looking and very you."

"Oh, a friend gave it to me a few days ago. It's unique and I love it. I always wear it now." This is when I hope George doesn't get curious.

"So, a friend gave you a ring and you wear it on your left ring finger? Interesting, why that finger?" Can I go now please?

"That's where it fits."

"And this friend, is he hot?"

Before my brain functioned and realized what George was up to, "Hotter than you can imagine." Shit.

George eyes the ring closely, "I see. It's very unique, like maybe somebody made it. Wait…" George turns back to his area and examines the bottle he has chilling to celebrate opening night. "That's from the top of a champagne bottle."

"Yea, he twisted it up and gave it to me. It's a memento from a big night. We celebrated with champagne when I was named Music Director."

"And, this hot guy that you haven't told me about kept the cage from the bottle, twisted it into a ring and gave it to you with absolutely no meaning at all, so you're never taking it off again?"

"Yep."

"You need to work on your story and do better next time. I'll let it go this time because it's opening night." I'll take it.

"Whatever you say, ma'am. I'll work on it." Happy I don't have to continue the interrogation. George finishes by adding a silver necklace with a large pendant around my neck. The pendant is about two inches across and it's a circle with a script letter J in the center, it lands right in the middle of my chest.

"Okay, put the vest on." George focuses on me, taking in every inch of my appearance and waits. "I like the vest, it really finishes the look. Go to Marni and then come back to me." George shoos me away.

I sit in Marni's chair and wait for her to do her magic. She does my make-up to make me stage ready and runs her fingers though my hair. She adds some long curls, pulling them through to keep them more wavy than curly and somehow by simply running her fingers through my hair she makes it shine with every strand in place.

I go back to George, "How does she do that? Marni's a witch or something. You look perfect, with just the right amount of shine and glisten for the stage." I blush at his words. "Okay, you're approved for the stage. Now, you do your job and make this place great. Have a great opening night." George high-fives me and sends me on my way.

I check on Katy, "Hey, I'm ready. How are you?"

"I'm happy to see that someone is ready. I'm not and there are people already outside waiting for the doors to open." Katy fakes a smile.

"What can I do to help?"

"Nothing. I need to breathe and trust the rest of the staff to do their job correctly on opening night. Do you have a gun?"

"Hold that thought." I go to the kitchen, grab a bottle of whiskey and return quickly to Katy's office. "No gun, but I have shots." I wiggle my eyebrows at her, suggesting that we do shots of whiskey from the bottle.

"You can't do shots, you're already in make-up. Give me that." Katy took a big swig straight from the bottle and rolled her neck around a couple of times. Then repeated the drink and roll process a couple more times.

When she sat the bottle down, I grabbed it and returned it to the kitchen. Danny caught me returning the booze, "What are you doing?"

"Uhhh, I found this and thought I should return it." I smile, I'm lying on purpose and not lying to him. "Just keep this bottle somewhere else. I have a feeling Katy may need it again soon."

"Got it. You look great, Jacks." Danny smiles at me.

"I'm already through make-up and wardrobe. I'm ready to do this thing. How about you?"

"Starting early made all the difference. Everything is going smooth. You sounded like a new person on stage earlier. I love the rock stuff you do. It's cool that you're being Jacks on stage, my Jacks." He winks at me and kicks me out, so he can focus on food preparation.

"Hey Katy, everything is going fine in the kitchen. All on schedule. I saw all the vocalists getting changed into wardrobe when I was leaving there. Everything seems to be smooth." Trying to alleviate some of the stress on Katy's shoulders.

"We're sold out for both seatings. Not an empty chair in the house tonight. Half were sold as whole tables. You might want to go out and greet guests that are waiting. See if you recognize any of them. Be personable and use your stage presence, consider it part of the show, introduce yourself and thank them for coming... blah, blah, blah. It's a job I would normally handle for the guys, but you should be the face tonight." Katy looks at me, proud and placing her trust in me.

"As you wish, Mistress Katy," comes out in an accent as I bow and go to work. I walk across the venue, smelling the deliciousness wafting from the kitchen, hearing everyone at work and the buzz of it all surrounding me.

I step up to the main entrance and examine the detail of the large, closed double doors. They're only doors, with the typical lit up green exit sign above them. They're stained solid wood with shiny brass hinges and they only open outward. I've never walked through these doors. I place one hand on each door and push through with gusto, pushing my way into my new life, my new career, my new home.

I hold the door, so it doesn't latch shut behind me and turn to the crowd that has gathered. It's got some familiar faces, "Welcome to the Supper Club! I'm Jacks and I'm the Music Director for the Supper Club. The whole team here has been working hard for weeks and we appreciate your support, especially on a night like tonight. Our opening night. We're all excited to get this going. The band is on point, the smells from the kitchen are to die for, and all eight of us vocalists will be performing for you. I'm your headliner tonight, so I'll be performing my whole set and I hope you love it. I was just told that we're sold out for both seatings tonight and we thank you all so much for making that happen. The doors will be opening soon. We can't wait for you to join us!" The crowd applauds and I smile uncontrollably as I survey the faces waiting to get in. Dot's beaming at me, full of pride, with her husband's arm wrapped around her. Joe and enough of my co-workers from the warehouse to fill two tables are standing toward the back of the group. Tony and half of the security team are hanging out, but seem to be doing more than observing. And, at least fifty other people that I don't know. I start to walk over to Dot, but I'm interrupted in the process.

"Jacks," Tony calls me over and I divert my route. "How's the chef doing?"

I love that Tony has Danny's back. "The kitchen is ready and on schedule. It smells amazing in there. He doesn't worry about Jackie when she's with her Uncle Tony. He's serving everyone a small sample of his new recipe tonight, Twice Fried Taters with Jacks Sauce. Don't worry about him, I made him take a break earlier. Danny is better than ready, everybody in Vegas is going to know who he is after tonight and want to eat at the Supper Club. He kicked me out of the kitchen a few minutes ago, so he could focus on service."

Tony grins at me, "Good. You look great and I can see that you're ready."

"Thanks, Tony. Hey, did mama bitch ever get home?" Not sure if I should be asking.

"No, but I checked with my security buddy at her work and she did clock in to work on time today. I'm hoping she goes home after work tonight. Otherwise, I'm off tonight and I'll cover if I need to. I'm hoping we all get to go out and celebrate opening night later."

"I like that idea. I've got friends here visiting, too." I wink at Tony and search for Dot.

Dot reaches for me and gives me a big hug as soon as I'm within her reach, "You look absolutely amazing! Beautiful!"

"Thank you. Thanks for coming. I hope you love the show. I'll visit with you after the show. I gotta make rounds here real quick and get back in there."

I walk up to the crowd of people in the far back that I know well from the warehouse and they cheer as I get closer to them, "Wooo! Jackie, Jackie, Jackie!"

"You guys are awesome! Thank you so much for coming and Joe especially. I really appreciate you. I'll see you all after the show. I hope you love it." I turn and walk back into the Supper Club, lighter, confident, and ready. I grab a couple Dr.

Pepper's from the kitchen quickly and stay out of the way. I find Katy and hand one of them to her, we pop open the cans and toast silently. Katy's better.

"Good job with the crowd. We'll be seating in a few minutes, so you should take a few minutes with your singers to get them pumped and ready, set some expectations. The guys and I will be wandering throughout the first show, so you'll see us backstage, in the kitchen, following servers, basically everywhere."

"I'm on it." I high-five Katy and gather my performers backstage. "Ladies, I'd like all of the vocalists on stage now please." There is some milling around, but no real action. "If you're performing tonight, you need to be on stage in 10, 9, 8, 7…" I continue the countdown and all of the vocalists are on stage before I get to 3. "Thank you. Tonight is a big night for all of us and we want to make a spectacular first impression. First of all, you all look gorgeous. Thank you George, Marni, Robyn, and Maria! My goal for us tonight is fun and professional. I'd like us to join the audience for a meet and greet after the show, together. Bond and make friends with each other, this is only the beginning." We're going to need water and hot tea backstage for the vocalists. "Chef, can we get some water and hot tea backstage for the vocalists, please. Kitchen, give me a woot if you got that."

"Woot!" Came from what sounded like the whole kitchen.

"Archie, we need a warm-up song. You guys got something that all of us know?" The vocalists glare at me like I'm crazy. "Better yet, I'm going micless on this and let's see who joins in. Arch, you guys have 'You Oughta Know' in your repertoire?" I turn to him with hope and watch as he gets nods from the band. "That Alanis Morrisette tune always gets me moving." Archie counts in the band and the drums start with some light snare, then I come in almost immediately on vocals. I wander the stage giving each of the vocalists attention and drawing them out to join me. I want all of us singing together and by the end of the song it's happening along with smiles and uncontrolled dancing. "Archie, throw something more Supper Club at us and let's see what happens." Soft bass starts and I give Archie an approving nod for 'Every Breath You Take' by the Police. I survey the faces around me and a few of the girls are already swaying, two of them come in with me right at the beginning of the song and the others all join in before the first chorus. Score! This is what we needed. At the end of the song, "Thank you, ladies. Make it a tradition before every show, whoever is singing that night should get together and sing a couple songs before the doors open. Even if I'm not here. Make sure you keep track of when you're on and don't leave the backstage area. Things happen and we need to be ready."

Katy and the guys are watching us, "Nice work, ladies," comes from Katy and all three applaud. They're happy with things so far. "Can you all gather together for me, please. We need some photos for advertising." The vocalists gather together in a half huddle facing Katy and she takes a few pictures. "Jacks, move to the center in front please and ladies, can you flank her in kind of a V formation. Perfect." She takes more photos. "Thank you. Let's do this. Curtains closed please. Floor staff, open the doors!" The sound of everything starting, doors opening, guests being greeted and seated, increasing my excitement.

I walk backstage and find Danny setting up a cart with water, hot water, tea bags, honey, lemon, sugar, a small bowl of fruit and some crackers with cheese. "Hey, sorry to put you on the spot."

"Katy had already mentioned to me that something would be needed backstage, so I ordered for it." Danny smiles at me with that smile of his that could end war, but mostly makes my tummy flutter and my heart beat faster.

"Thank you. Katy's the bomb." I survey my surroundings. I want to kiss him, but I can't because I'm stage ready. I lean into him and reach for his ear, "If I wasn't stage ready, I'd drag you to your office and have my way with you right now. You're so hot in your chef coat."

"Tease," he laughs, "Get to work, it's our night." Danny grabs my hand and kisses my fingers tenderly, then my palm with his open mouth and closes my hand before he turns to get back to work. There I stand, left all hot and bothered. All he did is kiss my hand. Fuck me. At least I know I have his kiss in the palm of my hand for extra support tonight. When did I become such a girl? Doesn't matter, I'm happy and I love it.

I spend a few minutes bonding with the band and go through their names a couple times to make sure I've got them down. Then I hang out backstage making sure my vocalists are ready and waiting at least a song early. Marni is running around touching up make-up and hair. George is giving everyone one last look-over before they walk out on stage, none of us will be on stage unless we're perfect to the eye. I prepare some hot tea and nibble on the cart that Danny has set up for us backstage. Note to self: Remember to eat ahead of time. The other vocalists are being more friendly with each other, even me. I start to hear the clattering of glasses and silverware, then the sound system comes on.

"Ladies and gentlemen, welcome to the Supper Club!" and went on to introduce each vocalist as they walked on stage to sing their short sets. Each vocalist gets applause, some more than others. I need to take notes on the audience reactions to songs and performers, so changes can be made.

CHAPTER TWENTY-FIVE

About halfway through the first show, Katy finds me, "Everything is going well. The audience loves the food, it's been getting served quickly and there's been no yelling in the kitchen. The band sounds great and the singers have all been at least good, some better than others. Are you ready to blow them all away?"

"Yea."

"Just yea?"

"I need to go sing in a corner somewhere or something and get pumped up. Being last is giving me time to come down."

"Danny's office used to be a walk-in freezer. It's mostly sound proof. Go! You have time. I'll hang here and make sure the last vocalists stay in line." Katy points to the kitchen.

I walk into the kitchen and call out to Danny, "Katy said to take over your office for a few minutes. Just letting you know." I walk into his office and close the door behind me. I stop and take a breath. I hum to myself and fall into "And I Love Her" by the Beatles. I'm warm and able, but not pumped. I go back to my audition and sing "Get Here" by Oleta Adams, then "Crazy" by Aerosmith and, finally, "Piece of My Heart" gets me where I need to be. My blood is flowing, my head is clear, music is running through me. I open the office door to find Danny leaning there, listening to me.

"You're ready, Jacks. Now, will you please get to work already?" He smiles at me and smacks me on the behind.

Backstage, George and Marni are both waiting for me. George makes sure everything is straight and where it belongs. Marni touches up my make-up and runs her magic fingers through my hair. The last song before my set is coming to an end. I was afraid I'd all of a sudden get nervous, that I might even pass out. Not the case, I can't wait to get my turn on stage. I gaze over at Archie and he smiles at me, pointing at me with an encouraging wink and letting me know I've got this. I've got this, Katy said I'm going to blow them all away, Danny said I'd rock it. It's on. The applause roars and the vocalist before me walks off stage. Then over the sound system, "Please welcome our Supper Club Music Director, Jacks!" I walk out on stage, communicating with the band before I go to the mic.

"Thank you all for coming. Can I get a big round of applause for the band? The Archies are doing a fantastic job tonight." I turn to the band smiling and clapping with the crowd. The keyboardist moves to the piano, he starts playing the clear, simple melody to "Get Here" and I start singing. I remember Danny's words, telling me how I'd pour my heart out there, it's exactly how I feel. I open up for the chorus and let it all go. I notice Katy, Danny, George, Marni and the guys all hanging backstage where they can watch, cheering me on, and clapping along with the audience. Dot and her husband are sitting near the front, she can hardly contain herself, beaming at me. Joe's two tables are making more noise than the rest of the room every time I finish a song. I manage to introduce the band correctly and people are moving to the dance floor, being moved by the music to be close and enjoy each other. It's an amazing sensation as I finish my set, the house is still full and they're standing on their feet. The room is filled with applause and I'm overwhelmed. I bow and throw a kiss out to the audience. The curtains close and I turn to Katy for direction as the cheering continues. She checks the time and mouths at me "one more, no band." I focus on her and think quick. The curtains open, "Thank you so much, you have no idea how much this means to me. I've been given permission to perform one more song for you. I hope you enjoy it and have a goodnight." I walk to the piano and tinkle across the keys lightly with the intro to "Don't Let the Sun Go Down On Me" by Elton John and bring in the bass a little heavier. Archie joins me with the tambourine. Then the drums and by the chorus the full band has fallen in. I build my vocals throughout the song, controlling the volume and the intensity. The band takes over the piano for me on the last verse and I concentrate on the vocals alone, taking them up a notch and letting my power rip. The song comes to an end and I'm more pumped than when I started, yet I'm out of breath. I place the mic on the stand and bow my head down.

The curtains close and Danny runs to me on stage, not caring who is around or who will witness his actions or who will find out about us, only caring about me and putting his arms around me tight, "You were fucking amazing, my Jacks." Tears rolling down my face and in my head the show's not done yet. There's another show tonight and I need to round up the other vocalists to meet and greet the audience. But, I need his support and I need him there to get me through this emotional moment. You might think I'm tired, worn out physically and emotionally from the long day. This is what I've been working for and I'm here. I'm taken by the pure happiness and nothing could make it better than Danny being there to share it with me.

"I'm not done yet, babe. I'm glad you were here with me

for this. I have more work to do and I'll come find you before the next seating. Love you," and I kiss his cheek. "Ladies!" I call out, "Are you ready to meet your guests?" Marni fixes my tear-stained make-up quickly and the other vocalists gather around me. We all walk out to the serving floor together and talk to anyone that wants to talk to us, thanking them for coming. Most of the crowd has gone, but my friends are at their tables waiting for me. I give Joe a big hug, the pride in his eyes evident. I greet all of my co-workers and everybody is raving about me and the food, especially Joe. Katy's not too far away from me, "Katy, this is my boss Joe. They'd like to compliment the chef, may I bring Danny out?"

Katy glares at me unsure, "Only if he has time. Second seating is coming up quick." I leave Katy to chat up Joe and run to the kitchen.

"Danny." His head pops around a corner. "Are you swamped or do you have a few minutes to spare?"

Danny walks over to me and whispers in my ear, "Anything for you, babe."

"How about for my boss, co-workers, and friends that were in the audience for our first seating?"

"Let's go." I grab Danny's hand and take him to the floor to meet everybody. Joe and my co-workers compliment him on the food.

Joe specifically asks Danny about the brownies, "Did the brownies work? Did they make blondie love you? If you were female, they'd make me love you."

Danny smiled, "I think she already loved me, but the brownies were inspired by her." Danny gazes at me adoringly.

"So, I'm guessing the Jacks Sauce wasn't named for the whiskey?" Joe pushes it. Danny shakes his hand and I swear he blushes.

"The flavor profile is sweet and smokey with a kick, does that sound familiar?" Danny laughs, "It's nice meeting you, sir." Danny's staring at me anxiously and I pull him away to meet Dot before he disappears into the kitchen.

"Hey Dot, this is Chef Danny."

"The Danny?"

"Yes."

Dot pulls me in close and whispers in my ear, "You're right, he's hot. I had no idea. Everything makes sense now."

Danny reaches to shake her hand, but ends up hugging her. "Your food was delicious. I could have eaten three of those brownies and that sauce with the fries was perfect." She holds on to his hand, "Make sure you take care of my girl, I think she'll be here permanently sooner than we know it."

"Thanks for keeping tabs on her when she's at home. I worry about her. I promise I'll do my best to take care of her. I hope she's here everyday, soon." Danny has that love-struck look in his eyes when he turns to gaze at me.

"I'll talk with you later, we have to get back to work." I turn with Danny and head back to Katy's office.

We both stare at Katy, "How'd we do?"

"I'm happy. The guys are happy. We didn't get one single complaint. I'm still waiting on the tips tally. Many compliments on the food. Everyone enjoyed the music, but you really did blow away the other singers, Jacks. I'm telling you personally, they didn't even compare to you. The guys wouldn't like this, but you could have your own show. I need you to work with the vocalists and make them better or we may need to hold another audition for you to find new vocalists."

"I was thinking I need to take some notes while they're performing. I'll do that during the second seating and meet with them all after the show tonight."

Katy shut her office door, "However, you two sucked at keeping your secret. What the hell?"

Danny and I glance at each other, "We'll do better. It's been an interesting day. We won't let it happen again."

"I don't care and the guys don't care. You two have proven yourselves with us. It's only you needing the secret." Katy leaves it at that for us to deal with. "Now, go do a repeat for seating two and plan on celebrating tonight."

Danny and I get back to work. I gather the vocalists backstage, "Ladies, I'd like you to discuss your performances and think about how you can make them better. I'll be taking notes during the second seating and will contact you individually."

CHAPTER TWENTY-SIX

The world was a wonderful place. The second seating went as planned and the vocalists were a bit better. I provided them notes and they took me seriously, practicing and showing improvement over the next couple of weeks. We had a great night out as a group celebrating and Danny stayed all night with me because mama bitch decided to go home after work, so it was a great night in, too.

The next couple of months went smooth, routine formed. I worked at the warehouse Monday through Thursday, and left early on Friday to drive to Vegas for the show. My Supper Club sets had increased, adding the two sets on Friday night and the Sunday night set. Five performances each week and they were still paying for my room. The extra money is great, but I'm still not ready to give up my day job. Danny was staying with me at the hotel at least one night every weekend and sneaking away with me for a "break" on long days. Mama bitch pulled her 'not coming home from work' stunt more frequently and had started to yell at Danny about him dating, even though he was always there to take care of Jackie and paid all of the bills, her money was free for her to use as she pleased—not to mention that they aren't a couple and never were. I know, they have Jackie, but one drunk fuck doesn't make you a couple. I've been on take Jackie to breakfast duty, spending time with her at the piano and showing her more music, even an afternoon in the arcade where we could sneak away for ice cream, always because she didn't come home when she knew Danny had work. I don't mind spending time with Jackie, I actually like it. We have fun.

Anyway, the Supper Club is going well. It's a success and both Danny and I are getting some notoriety. Katy is super happy with us, we've made her job easy. Her biggest concern is what the guys are coming up with to do next in their free time.

I miss Danny when I'm not in Vegas, but I love our phone conversations. It doesn't matter if it's thirty seconds and simply a chance to hear his voice or a whole hour talking about trivial everyday stuff or a drunk call or dirty talk for that matter. The sound of his voice, it's different inflections and tones, it makes me happy. We do have serious conversations, it's not all fun and games.

I've been considering moving to Vegas, giving up my room at the Stardust and asking for sets on Wednesday and Thursday. I'm pretty sure Joe would let me work from home doing sales if I go commission only. It would work and I wouldn't be worried about income. Danny wants me in Vegas every day, but the reality is that he doesn't want me to have my own place and live by myself. It was actually a fairly heated conversation, mostly because it makes him mad that he can't move in with me. It's the kind of guy he is. He wants to take care of me. It doesn't help that income wouldn't be an issue for me if we lived together, because we'd share expenses. And, I mean share expenses. He said he'd pay the whole rent and every-thing, but I don't work that way. It doesn't matter if you're roommates or a couple, you share expenses or contribute to the household needs equally somehow. It doesn't matter because he can't move out, he's stuck with mama bitch until he can find a way out with Jackie. I've considered finding a roommate, but I've never done well with roommates in the past and I like my space. I like my privacy. I want Danny over whenever he can be, and Jackie if that's possible. I may need to babysit.

There have been a couple incidents that have provoked mama bitch and made things more difficult for Danny. First, mama bitch had Jackie out at the mall and Jackie walked up to a keyboard and started playing. When she asked Jackie where she learned that, Jackie said, "Jacks shows me stuff when we go to breakfast and Daddy has to work." Which caused her to call Danny at work and go off on him, asking who Jacks is. I got the rundown from Katy because she could hear him yelling at her from her office, he told her, "If you were home to watch your daughter when you're supposed to be, so I can go to work, then I wouldn't have to take her to work with me and get help from my friends and co-workers. Maybe if you weren't drunk or on something all the time, you would enjoy time with your daughter and remember the few times a week that you actually need to be there for her. Everything I do is for Jackie, don't get any ideas that any of it's for you. It was never you and it never will be." Second, she found one of the hotel room keys I had given him. Then on a night when she didn't come home from work, she walked in around midnight and caught Danny on the phone with me. I have no idea how, but she somehow managed to listen to part of the conversation and when she saw his face she'd had enough. Danny told me he had to go, but didn't hang the phone up and nosey as I am I listened as she yelled and Danny didn't...

Her: You have the photo booth look on your face. Are you talking to her?

Danny: I'm allowed to be happy. You know I'm dating.

Her: You were talking all sweet and you called her Jacks! Are you having some girl you're dating babysit our daughter?

Danny: Jacks is not some girl I'm dating. She has helped me when I needed someone to watch Jackie at the last minute, because you weren't here like you were supposed to be. Jackie knows that Jacks is my friend and that's all.

Her: She's obviously more than that, I can see it on your face!

Danny: Stop yelling at me. Jackie doesn't need to hear you yelling and I'm tired of your shit. I don't ask you about what you do and with who, but you know what? I should because I don't want those drugged up losers around my daughter. The worst thing I've done is introduce my daughter to someone that she has fun with, that keeps her safe, that teaches her music and is willing to sacrifice part of her happiness to hide our relationship from the people around us and be a secret in my life, and I hate that she has to be a secret because of you. Jacks deserves better, but she does it for me. Jacks loves me and she loves Jackie, and you know what else? She'd be a better mom than you, if Jackie was only so lucky to have her. Huh? You know, if you weren't here Jacks would jump at the chance to be a family with me and Jackie. All three of us would be happier and you could go spend your nights with whoever you want, on whatever you want and not worry about taking care of your child.

Her: You're a fuckin' dick!

Danny: You asked the question. I answered it. And yes, Jacks is the girl from the photo booth. She's my one and only, she always will be. Anything else you want to know?

Her: You never gave me a chance. You've been with her this whole time. You lied to me. You said you were going to start dating a few months ago.

Danny: No. I didn't talk to her or see her for about three years. I ran into her on accident at the casino. I didn't lie and I'm not keeping her a secret any more.

Her: I hate you.

Danny: I'm tired of this. Jackie and I don't need you. We're fine without you, which is how we usually are. Now, get out of here and go sleep it off. You're obviously on something.

I hear her shuffle off and Danny hangs the phone up properly. I know I shouldn't have, but I couldn't help it and I called him back. He answered, "Jacks?"

"Yea, sorry to call, but I listened to the whole thing and I wanted to tell you that you're right. I would jump at being a family with you and Jackie. Good night," and I hung up.

I figure that these confrontations are happening more and more if I've been able to listen to one and Katy has, too. I feel bad for Danny, but I'm not letting him go. He wants to be us. I wish I could help bring someday to us sooner.

The weekend after I listened to the conversation that I shouldn't have, Danny didn't stay over with me because he isn't leaving Jackie alone with mama bitch any more. He worked and went straight home after every shift. On Sunday, when we didn't have to be to work as early, I met him and Jackie for ice cream. He's been trying to find a way to fix everything, he can't keep going the way he is. He's not telling me everything, but I trust him and he's doing what he thinks is best.

The phone conversations that next week are short, and I don't think anything of it. He has a lot going on.

When I get to the Supper Club on that Friday afternoon I do my normal routine, starting with leaning in the doorway of Katy's office, "Honey, I'm home!"

But, unlike the normal happy smart-ass response I've grown accustomed to over the last months, Katy is straight faced and hands me a bag, "I'm sure this is bad and I'm sorry. Remember that I'm only the messenger." I sit down in Katy's office and she closes the door. I open the bag to find a T-shirt, two boxes sealed up in plastic refrigerator bags and an envelope. I pull the T-shirt out and it smells like Danny. I open the envelope and pull out a notecard with photos in it. The card is light pink and says 'Someday' in ivory colored script, crayon style writing with a heart around it. There's a photo of us together from opening night, another of me and Jackie from a photo booth making silly faces, and a photo copy of his original photo booth strip of us. I open the card and it reads:

Jacks,

I'm pushing for someday to get here sooner. I'm sorry that means I won't be seeing you or talking to you for awhile. She came home late last night and went crazy. She said she can't live like this anymore. I was afraid she was suicidal or going to hurt us because I never know what's going on with her and the drugs she does. I called the police, they put her on a 72 hour hold and are going to have a psych evaluation done. I'm taking Jackie to my Mom's and I have a plan, but I don't know how long it will take. Know that I love you and only you. I'm not asking you to wait for me because I know that you will. I promise we will get our someday. I love you, Jacks.

Love,

Danny

The tears stream down my face and Katy hands me a tissue box. "This might not be the best time to talk about this, but Danny put in for extended family leave and I'm holding his position for him. He asked that I give you the set on Wednesdays and Thursdays, and if I would ask you to be my roommate—both only until he gets back. I'm happy to comply with his requests and I'd love to have you as a roommate. I know that's a lot all at once." Katy hands me my hotel room key and gives me a hug. "I'd give you the key to my place, but I think we're going to need a place to crash after we get drunk every night this weekend. Go get your stuff unloaded."

"He's already gone?"

"Yes, he was here this morning and we made a plan for ordering food, so I can handle that while he's gone. He had Jackie with him and they were leaving from here."

———

Somehow I made it through the next couple weeks without hiding under the blankets in the fetal position, but I don't commit to moving to Vegas or the extra sets. I stay in LA and keep my schedule the same. Mid week at home in LA I get a phone call, "Hello?" and I sound irritated, because lately that's how I sound.

"Hey Baby! It's Ron." I thought I'd lost Mr. Obnoxious. "My friends went to your show opening weekend and said you were awesome. I was at your show Saturday night and you were great, but seemed sad. Let me take you away from there."

"Hey, I don't know. Things aren't going well right now. I'm not in the mood for anything at all right now."

"Sweetheart, you need a change. I'm not kidding with you and I'm not trying to get in your pants. Honest, I'm trying to make some money on your talent. I can get you a show all to yourself Monday through Thursday to start. It won't even mess with your Supper Club schedule. It will get you in at the MGM and you can play whatever you want, it's your show."

"Did you say I can play whatever I want? Does that mean I can rock every song, every night if that's what I want?"

"Yes darling. Do I have your attention now?"

"Yes. Yes you do. I can change up the songs on the fly? I'll have a live band?"

"Of course. What other way is there?"

"I need to find a place and move to Vegas. Let me check with the Supper Club and make sure it won't be a problem. They've done a lot for me and I have good friends there."

"I understand, Katy told me to go to your show. That's just between you and me. Also, my daughter recently moved out and I have a one bedroom lock-out at my condo that she was using, you're welcome to use it."

"How about rent it? Does it have a kitchenette or anything?"

"Fine dear, $400 per month. It has a small kitchen area with everything you need."

"Thank you, Ron. Can I call you back in a bit? I appreciate the offer. By the way, how much would I get paid?"

"$800 per week for four shows, Sweetheart. Call me back," and he hangs up.

I walk around my apartment like a fool, not knowing what to do. Finally, I take a deep breath and call Katy.

"Hey," Katy answers the phone and it sounds like I caught her in the middle of something.

"Hey, do you have a minute because I just got an odd phone call that I'd like to ask your opinion on." I hear the background noise stop, she must've had me on speaker.

"Absolutely, what's up?"

"I got a call from that obnoxious performer guy, Ron. Are you familiar?"

"Yes I am. He's really a sweetheart in disguise."

"He offered me my own show at the MGM for Monday through Thursday and I can sing rock or whatever I want. Does that cause a problem with the Supper Club if I take his offer? What do you think?" I'd never be able to ask her this if he hadn't told me she clued him in.

"It doesn't mess with the Supper Club at all and I think it's a great opportunity. Make him pay you at least $600 for the week and have a clause added to the contract that he has to pay you an extra $50 every time he hits on you. He won't hit on you, but he'll like the idea of it. Also, make sure you get a year guarantee on the show."

"Okay, and what's your cut for being my manager?" I laugh.

"5%, I'm giving you the friends rate. I'm kidding, I'm happy to help. You can take me out to dinner after your opening night."

"Thank you. Katy, what do you think Danny will think about this?"

"I think Danny will be happy that you're doing something that you love, and he likes you doing rock best."

"Did you know I met Danny at Ron's show?"

"Really?" I could hear her wrinkling her nose through the phone.

"Yup. Ron called me and my friend, Jess, out to dance because nobody was dancing and then harassed the guys in the audience because they didn't join us on the dance floor. Then he called Danny and Tony out until they danced with us." I'm overwhelmed by happiness and tears at the same time, remembering the night and missing Danny.

"You gotta do it. It's meant to be."

"Thanks," I hang up and dial Ron.

"Hey Sweetheart," Ron answers the phone.

"I'm in. Can you get me a schedule? Enough time to give notice at my day job and to move?"

"Absolutely dear. I'll have a schedule and contract emailed to you tomorrow. We can chat then, okay?"

"Do you already have a band for me or can I recommend one?"

"I'm always interested in a new band. Can you get them here to play for me?"

"Yes, sir. Thank you," and I hang up.

I can't believe I'm going to do this. I call Bryan and he answers, "What's up?"

"Hey, can you come over? I'd like to talk to you about a couple of things. No sex or anything, but it might be better."

"Be there in ten minutes," and he hangs up.

I wander my apartment aimlessly. Thinking about how this is a good idea and a bad idea. I need to set everything straight. I love Bryan and I want him to succeed.

Bryan knocks on my door and I yell, "Come on in, Bryan."

"Hey, so what's up? I haven't heard from you in weeks. I know you're busy. I heard you're doing great in Vegas."

"Thanks." I lead Bryan to the couch and as always he has his guitar in his hand. "First, I need you to listen to everything and not get pissed, okay?"

"Okay," sounding hesitant.

"Good. This is about music. We've always been better together with music than any other way. I got offered my own show at the MGM and I'll be able to choose the music, change it up and everything. I'll have my own live band. My show will be Monday through Thursday. If we can be friends and not have issues with me having a guy or you having a girl, I can get you and your band an audition for the gig. I realize it's not what you want to do, but it wouldn't interfere with your weekend gigs. It will get you in front of more people and you'd get paid, so you could lose the day jobs or whatever the guys are doing to make ends meet. What do you think?"

"I'm in. Let me check with the band."

"Cool, and let me know when you can go to Vegas and play for Ron."

"We don't have a gig Friday night, but I'll let you know. We need to get a room, too."

"You can crash in my room at the Stardust on Friday night, but you'll be sleeping on the floor. It's free and that's for the whole band, not an invitation for you."

"So, what's up with the sex embargo?"

"I'm taken. I'm back together with my Vegas guy from a few years ago, and I don't need any judgment from you. Also, I have somebody I'd like to introduce you to. I think you'll totally click."

"Okay. Really? Him?"

"Yes." I show him the picture of the two of us from opening night and hold the photo booth strip back because he doesn't need to see us making out. But, he grabs it to look. He looks at us together and looks at me.

"He looks like he cares about you. I'll try to ignore it for now, best I can do."

"Fair enough. Wait until you meet Katy, she's a firecracker. You guys should come to the show Friday night. I'll be headlining and it'll give you a chance to watch me perform before you commit, but the music is a bit tamer than what I want for my show."

Bryan grabs my phone and makes a few phone calls. "Can we meet with Ron on Friday afternoon or Saturday morning? We want to do it."

I smile and ring Ron, "Hello darling, I didn't expect to hear from you so soon."

"I talked to the band I told you about. Can you meet with them Friday afternoon or Saturday morning?"

"Let's do Friday at 2pm. Have them meet me at my lounge in the MGM. My band will be there, so they can bring their instruments or not. Whatever works is fine. It's a short amount of time to set up drums and everything, but that's up to them. You think these guys are good?"

"They're better than good, you'll be blown away. I'll try to be there with them. Thanks, Ron."

I turn to Bryan, "How's 2pm on Friday?" I'm smiling from ear to ear for the first time in weeks. If I can only have half of my happy, then maybe Bryan can find his.

"Yes! I'll get us tickets for your show on Friday night, too. Thank you, Jackie. Or, should I call you Jacks?"

"Where did you hear that?" I stare at Bryan surprised that he'd heard about Jacks.

"You're getting more attention than you know. Is your guy the chef?"

"Yes, now you're freaking me out."

"There's a picture of you and him on the Supper Club

website and the photo you showed me looked familiar. You two are like a power duo."

I need to tell him the truth, "We could be if he didn't have issues with his daughter's mother. He's gone right now, but he'll be back." I say it and I believe it.

"You know I'm here if you need me." Bryan stops and gazes at me, "You know, you should call your show Jacks." He turns and walks out without so much as trying to kiss me.

CHAPTER TWENTY-SEVEN

I wake up early the next morning and check my email before I leave for work. I have the contract from Ron and a tentative schedule, so I'm not imagining things. I forward the email to Katy with a note for her to handle it since she's my manager, and to have them pay her direct, only partly kidding.

I park at work and my phone rings as I'm walking in. It's Katy, "Good Morning my love. Are you calling because you already read my email?"

"Hey crazy girl! Do you really want me to handle the contract for you? I've done it before and I can handle the manager role for talent."

"Yes. That way I can take you with me if I become famous. Did you review the contract? I'm getting ready to walk into my work at the warehouse and it would be good to know before I go in to talk to Joe."

"Geez, you're a demanding client. Then again the talent always is." Katy laughs. "I did a quick review, I've seen his contracts before and it's pretty standard. I'll have him add me as manager to pay me direct and the clause about $50 every time he hits on you."

"You're awesome. My friend Bryan is going to call in and get a table for his band for Friday night, can you make sure they get one of the better tables? Also, are you and Kyle a thing or are you available?"

"Bryan already called in, I'll check his table and switch it if necessary. I'm available, but Kyle doesn't like it. I'd be more available if they didn't keep me so busy."

"Cool, I want to introduce you to the band on Friday and you should hang with us after the shows on Friday night. I got them a meeting with Ron, I'm hoping they can be my band."

I hear Katy's brain, "Are you sure that's a good idea?"

"No, but I did it anyway. We talked about it and they're the best band I know. They play more my style and they know me. Plus, it won't interfere with their weekend gigs. I'm going for it. In fact, can I bring Bryan on stage with me Friday night to play guitar for me for a song or two, change up my set a little?"

"Now you're pushing it lady. I'll check with the guys, but it shouldn't be a problem. You need to ask Archie though, so you don't step on any toes."

"Cool. I need to ask Bryan what he thinks of the idea anyway. Can you email me Archie's number, too? Okay, I gotta go talk to Joe. Have a great day and I'll bug you later," I hang up.

Deep breath, I walk into Joe's office. "Hi Joe. What do you think about me changing to commission sales only and working from home?"

Joe stops what he's doing and focuses on me from behind his desk, "What's going on now?"

I smile, "I got offered my own show at the MGM Monday through Thursday. But, I can still do my phone sales and I can go out to our clients in the Las Vegas region to develop those clients."

"I'm proud of you, kid. Way to hustle and make it work. You should quit and move on."

"No, I like it here and I don't want to leave. But, I need to move to Vegas and I can't manage the commute. I appreciate your support and it gives me a back-up plan. If you replace me and want me to quit, I get it. But, at least let me do sales until that happens, and I expect to see you at my opening night at the MGM even though it'll be during the week."

"You got it. Any schedule change for this week?"

"Oh yeah, I need off Friday because I'm taking a band with me to Vegas to audition to be my show band. I'll have the rest of my schedule for you on Monday, my manager is handling the show contract for me. Thank you, Joe." I walk out of his office happy and get to work.

I find Bryan at my truck with lunch when I walk out on my lunch break. "Hey, I wanted to thank you for thinking of me and the band."

"No worries, Bry. I got Friday off, so I'll be there to introduce you guys to Ron. I was thinking, would you like to join me on stage as my special guest Friday night? Maybe a song or two with your acoustic?"

"Absolutely," Bryan gives me a big smile.

"Cool, I already asked and I'm waiting to get an okay. I need to check with Archie, so we aren't stepping on his toes. It shouldn't be a problem. Come up with a couple songs for us and maybe we can practice later at my place?" My heart is at least halfway happy, but it makes me think about the other half and I dial Katy while I inhale my lunch.

"Seriously? You're high maintenance. I'm going to increase my cut. What's up?" Katy sounds like she's had too much coffee.

"I'm on my lunch break and want to check in with you. I'm off Friday, so let me know if you want me there Thursday night for anything. Umm, any word from Danny?" Bryan turns, listening attentively to my conversation.

"FYI Thursday is tomorrow, some girl time would be nice since there's only one show and I can sneak away. Nothing from Danny."

"Okay, just felt like I should ask. I'll be there tomorrow night then," and I hang up.

Bryan stares at me, "Are you okay?"

"Yea, everything will be fine in time. Besides, I have a show," I remind myself constantly because it's better than pouting and wandering around like a dead person. I'll get my Danny back. "I have to get back to work. Thanks for lunch."

"I'll be by later," he calls to me across the parking lot.

CHAPTER TWENTY-EIGHT

I started laundry and got packed as soon as I got home from work Wednesday, so I'd be ready to go and be able to spend some music time with Bryan. It was great to spend a few hours singing with him.

Thursday went quickly and I took off for Vegas in time to spend the evening with Katy. She's turned into one of the best friends I have, I love her to pieces—especially smart-ass mode. We both need girl time sometimes. Tonight she scheduled us spa time. Yes, spa time. I mean the works. Manicure, pedicure, ninety minute couples massage, facial—the works. Best almost three hours ever. Even better, Katy made Kyle and James pay for it.

Friday morning I do something that I haven't done in months, sleep in. No alarm clock to wake me up. No work to be at. Nowhere to be until 2pm. So, of course my phone rings at 10am, "Hello, sleeping in today so make it good," without opening my eyes or even checking the caller ID. But nobody says anything. I force myself to open my eyes and look at the caller ID. I don't recognize the number. I don't even know the area code and that's when it hits me, "Danny?" and the phone disconnects. Probably a wrong number and me wishing it was Danny. I pull the blankets up over my head and go back to sleep, really considering the fetal position. 11:30am and my phone rings again, "Hello?"

"Hey lazy, bring lunch. Preferably pizza from that place a couple blocks over. I'll call in the order, you go get it and pay." Katy's in boss mode and that's never good on a Friday.

"Sure thing," as I open my eyes and sit up.

"Good, because I already ordered and it'll be ready in twenty minutes. So, get up!"

"I'm going," and I hang up. Rolling out of bed I think about what I'm going to put on. I'm going with the band to meet Ron and I want to make a good impression, but at the same time I'm a rocker. I pull on my tight ripped jeans and my boots up over my knees. I shuffle through the clothes I brought with me and choose my black sleeveless drapey top. I check my reflection in the mirror and I need some pop. I need accessories, I'll hit up George. I brush out my hair and leave it down straight. I grab my necessities and run out to pick up pizza.

I get to the Supper Club with pizza. Nobody said anything about the order being four pizzas, but I went with it and covered the bill. "Delivery," I call out as I walk into Katy's office.

"This is why I love you," Katy says to me and takes the pizzas away from me.

I grab a slice and inhale it as my phones rings, "Hello?" with my mouth full.

"Hey Jackie, should we meet you somewhere and go to the MGM together? We're rolling into town now," Bryan wants everything to be perfect and I don't blame him.

I check the time, "We have some time. Stop by the Stardust and come find me at the Supper Club."

"On our way."

I finish my slice and find George, "Georgie, can you fix me?"

George leans back and examines at me, "You did pretty good today considering you have to wear those boots and love ripped jeans." He fixes my top to make it hang properly and grabs my hippie glasses out of my accessory bin, sliding them up onto my head. Then he disappears and comes back with a belt made of shiny silver rings and puts it around my waist low, almost more around my hips. He also pulls the bangle bracelets from my bin and slides them over my hands. "That'll do. I heard you have a new gig, you deserve it. Don't forget us." George smiles at me. "Go see Marni and have her do your face."

I turn and she's waiting for me, "How about some day make-up and I'll make you stage ready later?"

"Sounds good." Marni gives me more eyeliner than she does on stage and really captures me, "Thank you, ma'am. It's perfect."

I walk out on stage as Bryan's walking into the Supper Club, "Hey Bryan, I'll be right there." He waves at me. I get to the floor and lead him back to Katy's office, "Katy, this is Bryan. I'm going over to meet Ron with him and the band. I'll be back in plenty of time for the show tonight."

"Nice to meet you. Stay out of trouble crazy girl and don't be late," Katy shakes her head as I turn to leave, but she's definitely checking out Bryan as we walk away.

"Do you guys have a room or are you crashing with me?"

"Crashing with you."

We get their stuff up to my room and take off for the MGM. "Bryan, you seem quiet."

"You're different here. I don't know, more confident or something. It's not a bad thing." Interesting that he thinks that.

We park at the MGM and I lead the way into Ron's lounge. We walk in and sit down while they finish their practice. Ron waves at me and calls me up on to the stage. "Johnny, you and the guys gotta hear this chic wail. You up for it, Jacks?"

"Always. Bring it."

"Do 'Piece of My Heart' and then hit her with some Aerosmith." Ron makes it easy and I realize Bryan hasn't seen me do this. I watch as Bryan and his band exchange glances with each other as soon as I hit the chorus on "Piece of My Heart." I get approving nods from Ron along with his obnoxious grin. It's exhilarating to rock that song harder. The band goes with "Angel" for the Aerosmith, it gives me an opportunity to show my range, like most Aerosmith songs do, and I let loose. Bryan and his band are on their feet clapping and Ron's band have hands outstretched to receive high-fives.

"That rocked, guys." I turn to Ron for the next step as I try to maintain control of my stage high after getting to hit it hard live. "This is Bryan, you want to introduce the rest of the band?" I let Bryan take over from there and lay low, so I don't distract anybody.

Ron walks over to me, "These guys are good. Where did you find them?"

"I've been singing with Bryan in my living room for years."

"He sings?"

"Yeah and he writes songs, too. He's good. May I?"

"Go for it." Ron gestures for me to take the stage.

"Hey Bryan, can you grab that acoustic and join me center stage?" Trying to think quick and come up with a song that we sing together in my living room. I pull two stools together and whisper to Bryan, "What do you want to play that we sing together, duet style or harmonizing. Just like in my living room. Beatles? Mr. Big? Extreme? You pick and I got your back on whatever you choose." Bryan nods and starts to strum his guitar for "To Be With You" by Mr. Big, I take the lead on the first verse, clapping along. We switch parts at the second verse, each singing the background part for the other and then harmonizing on the last verse. Ron signals me to do another one. I flash him a two, so we can do two more, getting an approval. I whisper to Bryan, "We get two more in this format, let's do 'High Enough' and a Beatles your choice, yeah?" Bryan nods and starts in on "High Enough" by Damn Yankees, which was made for two voices. Then he immediately moves on to his Beatles choice, "We Can Work It Out" and I grab a tambourine. We sing the whole thing together and harmonize on the chorus. I high-five Bryan when we're done and move off the stage. I stand next to Ron and try to stay out of the way.

"Hey kid, you can sing. I like it." Ron nods.

I lean to Ron, "They play gigs on the weekends, you should hear what they usually play."

"Give me a couple from your regular weekend gig," Ron calls out.

Bryan gives them a signal and they start in playing three of their best, a couple of covers and one of Bryan's originals.

Ron glances at me, "I like these guys."

"That's why they're here. What do you think? Can they be my band?"

"Baby, they might be too good for your gig. But, everybody starts somewhere and maybe it's a good step for them. You want them? There's five of them, I can only do $2000 for the band total to start. Maybe they can pick up something else, too. You tell them."

"Alright," I walk out on the stage and talk to Bryan, giving him the details.

"Let me talk to the rest of the band and give us overnight to figure it out, okay?"

"No problem. I want you guys here, but only if it'll work for you. It's the same pay even if there are only four of you." I walk back to Ron, "They'll let me know tomorrow. I feel good about it. Do you need anything from me? I need to get back to the Supper Club."

"No darling, have a good show tonight. Good find on the band." Ron waves me out and the guys follow me out, back to the Stardust.

CHAPTER TWENTY-NINE

I walk into Katy's office, "I'm back. Ron liked the band. I'm off to find Archie and get ready for the show. Need me for anything?"

"Just your love and devotion, sweetheart. Go get ready for the show." Katy kicks me out of her office and I handle business.

"Archie, do you mind if I have a friend on stage to play and sing with me for a couple songs tonight?"

"I'm good with that. Bring him by to meet us pre-show."

"You got it, thanks."

I visit with George and Marni quickly, and I'm stage ready. George doesn't make me change, and I think that could be a first. Marni fluffs out my hair and makes it shiny with her magic. The other vocalists are roaming around backstage. I bring Bryan up on stage to meet Archie and the band, while the other vocalists and I work through our pre-show routine. Archie calls me back and wants to hear Bryan and I do a song before the show. I turn to Bryan, "We can't do Beatles because I have a medley in my set. How about Mr. Big and Damn Yankees like earlier and 'We Can Work It Out' now?"

"Let's do it." Bryan nods and grabs his guitar.

"Good evening everybody, this is a test. Please welcome my friend, Bryan. He'll be joining me on this next tune." Bryan starts in on guitar and we do exactly what we did earlier, but the sound system is on in the Supper Club and the mics are live. Bryan is into it and inspired. Archie gives us his stamp of approval and Bryan goes off to find the rest of the band.

The shows on Friday night go well. It's refreshing to have Bryan join me on stage and if I'm not mistaken, Katy enjoyed that part of the show.

I keep wandering into the kitchen for no reason. I'm not grabbing a soda. I'm not taking over Danny's office to get pumped up for the show. I'm not wandering through in search of food I can steal to munch on. I'm simply drawn to the kitchen and I don't know what or who I'm searching for, but it isn't there. The smells of his recipes being prepared, his chef coat hanging in his office, the prep schedule on the big white board in his writing. Yea, signs of his presence are here, but not him. I'm overwhelmed by everything reminding me of him at the same time. Hot tears stream down my cheeks and I hide in his office to get a few minutes of recovery time to myself. I sit in the chair at his desk and I instantly start to bawl like a little girl when I notice his photos of Jackie and him together. I smell his scent. I want to wrap myself in his chef coat, but that would make me seem crazy. Well, truth is that I am. I'm crazy for Danny. I tell myself I made it three years, this will be a cakewalk. But, it doesn't feel like it. My heart is tearing apart more each day. I want to go to my room and hide under the blankets, but the band is crashing with me tonight and they can't see me like this. I look up and see a member of the kitchen staff pointing me out to Katy. Katy walks toward me and I yell out, "Why won't he call me?" as I cry.

Katy picks up the phone and dials the hotel operator, "Get me walkie 4." She waits a second, "I have a problem in the

Supper Club kitchen. No other back up needed." Katy hangs up abruptly. "Sweetie, I'm sorry and I don't know why he hasn't called. But, I know he loves you and he'll be back."

Tony walks in quickly, "What's wrong?"

Katy points at me, "Your boy is upsetting my girl. She wants to talk to him, she doesn't understand why he hasn't called, she wants to know what's going on, she wonders how long he'll be gone and as you can see, she loves him and misses him." Katy takes a breath and checks with me, "Did I miss anything?" I shake my head unable to speak through my sobs. We both focus on Tony like he's going to perform magic.

"I can't stand seeing girls cry." Tony shakes his head. "He loves you, Jacks, and he'll be back."

Katy starts in, "Nice work, slugger. I already covered those points. What else have you got?" and stares at him expectantly. "Have you talked to him since he left?"

"No. I have a phone number for him, but he said only to call if it's an emergency." Tony stares at us like this isn't an emergency.

Katy takes control, "We want to know why he can't make a quick phone call and we want to know now." She nods her head to add conviction.

Tony rubs his temples, "Jacks, let me walk you to your room and get you something to eat. You can get some rest and it'll be better in the morning."

"I can't go to my room like this. How will it be better in the morning? Will Danny be here?" I'm barely able to speak coherently.

"You are strong and just tired, tomorrow will be a new day. No, Danny won't be here tomorrow." Tony tries to placate me.

Katy gets a questioning expression on her face, "Are you sure he won't be here tomorrow? Did he tell you when he's coming back?"

"He doesn't know yet. He's still waiting on paperwork."

Katy gives Tony an evil stare, "So, he has talked to you?"

"Shit. I'm helping him with some stuff here."

"And now you're going to get him on the phone to talk to Jacks." Katy puts her foot down.

"Ladies, you don't understand. He's not calling on purpose. He doesn't want to make it harder by calling and he remembers what it was like years ago when he couldn't see you."

I'm furious, "Stupid fucking boys! We're a team. He needs to talk to me. I can help. I'm not going anywhere. This is different than before. We thought it was over then and he was marrying mama bitch, but now there is no over. This is our beginning and we have a someday!" I realize I'm probably not being helpful, but, "Call him now and tell him."

"Jacks, it's like 5am on the East Coast."

"Good, maybe he'll be up." Why yes, you will find a picture of me next to the word obstinate in the dictionary.

Tony turns to Katy for help, but doesn't get it, "You heard her. Call him."

Exasperated, Tony picks up the phone and dials, "Good morning, ma'am. Sorry to wake you. May I speak to Danny? Not sure it's a real emergency, but I have an extremely distraught woman who's demanding to talk to him." Tony listens and responds, "Yes, she loves him and she's beautiful. He's probably missing her and doesn't want to admit it. Trust me, I know how he gets when he can't be with her. Been there, done that. Ma'am, please tell him to stop torturing himself and get on the phone." Tony looks down and shuffles his foot across the floor, "Good morning. Why won't you call your woman? She's sitting in your office and she's a wreck." Tony doesn't even wait for a response he hands me the phone.

I interrupt Danny mid sentence, "Hi." It's all I can manage and not sound like a fool.

"Jacks, baby. I miss you so much." Danny's voice makes my heart warm.

"Why didn't you call? I thought we were a team, only us." I ask with a shake in my voice. Katy and Tony leave, closing the door behind them.

"It will always be only us, my Jacks. I didn't want to make it worse by calling and reminding you that I'm not there. I didn't mean to upset you, baby. I need to handle the situation and I did what I thought I should do."

"You could've called me. Maybe I could've helped. But, I don't know where you are and I don't even have a number to call you. We're a team, Danny. This isn't like before. I get it, we thought it was over and talking when we could never be together again was drawing out the torture. Now, huh, now you are never getting rid of me. There's nobody that can keep us apart," then a horrible possibility crosses my mind, "Unless you ran off for another girl." I'm overwhelmed by sadness at the idea and the tears roll again.

"Jacks baby, there's nobody else. Don't even think that. You're right, it's different because we're together now. I'm used to handling things for me and Jackie. I'm sorry baby, you're part of us. I love you, Jacks."

"When are you coming home?"

"I don't know yet. I need to get this taken care of for Jackie and then I'll be back to you. If it goes as planned, we'll be a step closer to our someday. I'm sorry, hold on a second..." then I can hear him talking to his Mom, "Yes, mom," he sighs, "I love her, really. You'll meet her eventually. Jackie thinks she's great. I'll show you pictures after I hang up. Mom!"

"Sorry, mom was listening in over here and now I'm in trouble because I didn't tell her I have a special girl."

Suddenly I feel better and my smile breaks through, "Tell me about your special girl," I giggle.

"Jacks, my mom is right here listening."

"It's okay, she won't mind," I laugh at myself, completely happy for the first time in weeks.

"You're my only girl, Jacks. There's never been anybody else, only you. I have the cork right here in my pocket and you know I plan to replace that champagne cage with something real. We're real baby."

I realize that I have news to share, "So, I have a couple things to tell you. I'm moving to Vegas and Mr. Obnoxious offered me a show of my own where I can rock. I really wanted to tell you, but I didn't know how to reach you. Is it okay if I call the show Jacks?"

"That's awesome, Jacks. You should call it Jacks. Are you moving in with Katy?"

"No, I got my own place. It's a one-bedroom lock-out at Ron's. Also, I need to talk to you about my band. Um, I got Bryan's band an audition with Ron and they're going to be my band for my show. I already told him I'm with you and I'm going to attempt a love connection with him and Katy. I want you to know, he's just my music buddy." I wait for his response.

"That guy that was at your door at 2am, him?"

"Yes. He's only a friend and a great musician."

"I trust your judgment, Jacks. You need to have the best musicians."

"And the whole band is sleeping on the floor in my room tonight. They didn't have money for a room and I wanted them to audition." It wasn't the best idea, but I wanted them for my band and it worked.

"I'm not a fan, but it makes sense. Get Katy to stay with you tonight, too. Tell her you like to be spooned. I have no problem with her in my spot of the bed with you."

I laugh, "I miss you so much that I can't even explain. I kind of lost it tonight, I started wandering the kitchen and ended up sitting at your desk. I'll survive, but it won't be okay until you're here with me," my voice low and sincere.

"Me too, Jacks. Me too. I'll call you. I need to go before

my mom takes the phone from me to talk to you. Love you, baby," and he hangs up.

I open Danny's office door to find Katy and Tony standing there waiting. "Better?" Katy asks me.

"Yes. Thank you." I'm happy and tear stained.

"You two are dangerous together," Tony says glaring and pointing at Katy and I. "The world doesn't know the power you have, but I'm beginning to think that you do."

Katy and I gaze at each other with evil grins and bust out laughing. "Thank you, Tony." He walks away as quickly as possible.

I remember my conversation with Danny, "So, can you stay with me tonight?" I ask Katy sheepishly.

"Do I want to know why?" Always untrusting.

"Danny wants you to stay with me. He said to tell you that I like to be spooned. And, he wants you with me so I'm not in the room with the band alone." I wait expecting to get a reaction.

"Bryan and his band are crashing in your room, and you want me to stay with you and spoon you?"

"Yep, and so does Danny. I told them they could sleep in my room, but it would be on the floor. Danny wants to make sure none of them take his spot, but he's fine with you sleeping in his spot. Besides, it'll be fun and you can get to know Bryan. You heard him tonight. He's talented and cute, right? I need to talk them into being my band for the money Ron offered them, too. You can probably help with that. Oh! You should be their manager, they're going to be huge."

Katy lets out a long exasperated sigh, "Fine." She stops to think, "Can we make sure Kyle knows we're spending the night with the band? It'll drive him up the wall." I nod enthusiastically and help Katy close up the Supper Club for the night.

We walk into the casino and find the band watching a lounge

act, well critiquing is more like it. I introduce Katy as my manager and tell them they should get her to manage them, too. Katy rolls her eyes, but goes along with it. "If you don't approve of this band, why don't we go to the room and you guys can play?" I suggest. Katy needs to witness what the band has to offer.

We all get back to my room and Bryan goes straight for his guitar. I grab my sweats and Danny's Skid Row T-shirt, and run into the bathroom to change. I come back to find Katy watching and listening contently, and I catch a glimpse of what Bryan does to every female on the planet. Katy isn't bullet-proof. Bryan keeps playing and the drummer starts beating sticks all over. Bryan switches it up and starts in on some Beatles, that's my queue to join them and I can't help myself. Bryan is singing and the other guys add back-up vocals. I catch Katy backing to the corner of the room and taking in the scene as a whole, her mind is working.

During a break in the music, "Have you decided if you're going to take the gig at the MGM?" Katy turns to Bryan and the band. She physically stops, "Do you guys have a name?"

"The Consequences." Bryan responds to Katy's quizzical expression, "Sometimes we write about the aftermath and other times we're the consequences of the situation. Really, isn't that what love songs are about? Music is mostly reflection on times in our life and our emotions." Well, if Katy wasn't hooked on Bryan yet, she is now. I mean what male has that emotion available and puts it out there? Luckily, he's in control of it and not going overboard with it.

"Jacks and the Consequences, interesting. I like it." Katy states bluntly.

Bryan looks down and under his breath, "Some of my songs are just the opposite, the consequences of Jacks." He gazes up at me and catches my eyes with his.

"Only the one song," I correct him.

"No, there are others. You've heard them, you just didn't know they were inspired by you." Bryan refuses to let it go.

"Any that you want to share now?" I stare at him wondering what others are because of me.

Bryan stops and communicates silently with the other guys, the drummer starts a beat on his thighs and the other guitarist starts a rhythm going. Bryan adds melody with his guitar and I'm happy to hear it's upbeat. Bryan starts singing:

That girl,
She keeps me on my toes,
That girl,
She leaves me wanting more,
That girl,
Her smile lights up the world,
Oh, that girl!

But she's so cruel,
She don't need you,
You're just her fuel,
Lucky she'd use you,
And she don't even know,
What she does to me, oh,
Yeah, she don't even know.

That girl,
She makes me so happy,
That girl,
She makes me feel sappy,
That girl,
Wish she'd call me daddy,
Oh, that girl!

But she's so cruel,

She don't need you,
You're just her fuel,
Lucky she'd use you,
And she don't even know,
What she does to me, oh,
Yeah, she don't even know.

That girl,
You take what you can get,
That girl,
She's bound to make you sweat,
That girl,
She goes straight to your head,
Oh, that girl!

But she's so cruel,
She don't need you,
You're just her fuel,
Lucky she'd use you,
And she don't even know,
What she does to me, oh,
Yeah, she don't even know.

That girl,
She's a bet you want to take,
That girl,
She'll make your heart ache,
That girl,
Hope she's there when I wake,
Oh, that girl!

But she's so cruel,
She don't need you,
You're just her fuel,

Lucky she'd use you,
And she don't even know,
What she does to me, oh,
Yeah, she don't even know.

That girl!

Bryan's right, I've listened to the Consequences perform that song many times and had no idea. I've always loved that one and the percussion-clapping sound of the "That girl" lines, as well as the rhythmic timing. Katy turns to me, "Do you run around breaking hearts or what?"

Bryan comes to my rescue, "No, she doesn't know what affect she has on people. It's what makes her so special, that she doesn't think she's special. Even now, she's been performing at the Supper Club, she's got her own show now, and what does Jackie do? She doesn't get mean or uppity. She calls me and gets us a steady paying gig. She brings me on stage with her. She wants everybody to be happy and doesn't let her own sadness get in the way of helping friends." I turn to Bryan a bit stunned. "I know you've been upset all week and I can see you've been crying, but seem to be okay now. I know there's something going on with you and your boyfriend. I don't like that he's making you upset, but I respect your decisions."

Right then my phone rings and I answer, "Hello?"

"Hey Jacks. I wanted to call you, to make sure you have the number here." I can hear him smiling through the phone.

"Hey baby!" As soon as Bryan realizes I'm talking to Danny, he starts playing and singing "You're Going to Lose That Girl" by the Beatles like it's a message. "That makes me feel better, I won't call too often." I take the call out to the hall.

"Where are you?"

"I was in my room with the band and Katy, practicing with acoustics. I moved out to the hall, so I can hear you."

"The worst part of this is that I want to be with you and take care of you. I've been thinking about what you said earlier, and you're right, I should've called you first. I'm sorry I left like that."

"I understand, Jackie needs to be your priority. I can take care of myself."

"Damn it! I know you can take care of yourself, but I want to take care of you. I need to be able to take care of both of you. Jacks, don't you get it?" Danny stops and I can hear his frustration in his breathing, "I want to do things that make you happy. I want to give you everything you want. I want to provide you with everything that you need. I want to cook special recipes for you and create recipes around you, so you keep making those noises when you eat my food. I want to please you. I want to see your face, taste your lips, hold you and wake up with you everyday. I'm your man and I want you to know it in every way. You'll always be you, Jacks. I need you to know I'm there for you, however it is that you need me to be there."

I love his words and his intensity, but suddenly I'm mad at him for not being here to take care of me, and all the things he said. I can't listen to this until it's real. "Danny, I love you, but I, I can't listen to this and believe it in my heart until you're here with me, until it's real. I know you love me. I'll be here when you get back. I'm not trying to pressure you, I really do understand that Jackie needs to be your priority. I guess I'm kind of like you doing what you know and taking care of Jackie because it's just what you do. I take care of me because nobody else ever has."

"Jacks. That's not what I... I don't know how to explain. It tears me up because I'm not there doing those things. Please don't give up on me, don't give up on us."

"I need to focus on music and the show anyway. I'll be waiting for you. I'm going to be busy moving. I need to get back in the room, I left Katy with the band," It's an excuse and I notice the music has stopped.

"Don't be like that, Jacks. Don't shut me out. Please, don't shut me out."

I walk back into the room to find the band lying on the floor with makeshift pillows. Bryan's sitting at the foot of the bed talking to Katy. Katy's lying on the bed, "Sweetheart, is that you? Come over here so I can spoon you." Bryan shakes his head and finds a space to crash, he actually kicks his drummer and takes his spot when the drummer goes off to sleep in the tub. The other guitarist slides the closet door open and rolls in there to sleep.

"Yay!" I climb in bed, "Snuggle up close."

"Freak," Katy laughs and we go to sleep.

CHAPTER THIRTY

I wake up the next morning and spooning had turned into sharing a pillow with our arms around each other. "Wow, I thought the problem was the boyfriend, but now I'm not sure. Something we should know about, ladies?" Bryan and the rest of the Consequences are standing at the foot of the bed staring at us. Katy and I immediately separate and sit up.

I wink at Katy, "Ain't nothing wrong with some girl love," and she laughs at me. The guys are packed up and ready to get back to LA for their gig tonight.

Katy pipes in, "You can't leave yet. There's business to handle." Bryan rolls his eyes and sighs. "And, that's exactly why. You don't like to handle the business part of it. You need me. You need to contract me to be your manager and I'll handle the negotiations and contracts for your gigs."

"We can't afford a manager." The drummer speaks.

"You can't afford not to have me. I'll make you a deal, long ten year contract, and you don't pay me until you break $40k per year. That's based on each of you individually, so I expect that Bryan will have to pay first since he writes music, too. Meet me in my office in thirty minutes and I'll have the paperwork ready. What do you want from the contract for Jack's gig?" Katy's all business in a matter of seconds and jumps out of bed, fixing her hair before they can even answer.

"The gig pays fine for us, if we didn't need to find a place to stay while we're in Vegas during the week. Obviously, we'd like it to be more. You always wish your job paid more." The band nods in agreement.

"Can you share a room that long or do you require separate quarters? Do you care where you stay?"

"We can share, but five of us with one bathroom is pushing it. We need a place that's clean and safe to leave our gear."

Katy takes off, yelling back as she leaves the room, "My office in thirty minutes, be there."

Bryan turns to me, "Is she serious?"

"Yup. Katy is magic when it comes to business. I suggest you take coffee and donuts." The band communicates silently with each other and nods in agreement, then leave.

I lie back down in bed and pull the blankets up around my neck. I haven't had any time to myself since my incident in the kitchen last night. Now that I've talked to Danny and he actually called me again, I'm relieved that he's okay. I can't believe he managed to piss me off for the first time and he's on the other side of the country. It could be that my patience for this is wearing thin, but that's never been a problem before. It's not a problem when he's here, his presence distracts me. None of it matters. I still have no idea when he's coming back. I don't like thinking about the comparison to when we were apart before, but I focused on the only other thing that makes me happy, music. And, guess what? It worked. I'm finally doing what I want to do and moving forward. I'll be living on singing very soon. I have my own show. I have my own band. I get to pick the music. I'll be performing every night of the week. Vegas is the right place and it seems I may have found the right time. So, I'm going back to the old plan—focus on the music.

Maybe Danny was right, it's better not to talk while he's gone. He doesn't need to be included in everything. He'll catch up when he gets back. What's the difference? I didn't get to share my excitement with him when it happened. He didn't need to talk to me before he left. Maybe he doesn't need to talk to me. Maybe he doesn't need me. Sadness rolls over me and I refuse to let it take over. Fuck that! I've got shit to do. I jump out of bed, shower, get dressed and go to Katy's office.

"Good morning my love, the bed was so cold without you," I laugh at Katy from her office doorway.

Katy shakes her head at me, "Hey crazy. The band is good to go. I'm their manager and I already handled the MGM gig. You have a band." I do a little dance and twirl around. I needed some good news.

"Yay! I'm going to check the apartment Ron has for rent. Can you get out of here and go with me?" Katy nods and we get out of the Supper Club for a bit.

Turns out the apartment is perfect. Ron's going to have the furniture moved out and get it cleaned for me. I can move in a few days. Katy and I pushed the time out of the Supper Club, enjoying a nice lunch out.

The Archies indulged me pre-show on Saturday and helped me get it all out. I needed to sing. I needed to rock it. I needed to release all my pissed off girl anger. Archie picked up on the songs I wanted and kept throwing the same thing out there. Each song angry, or with a driving beat, or hating an ex, or telling the significant other to tread lightly, or asking the question if it's over or establishing independence. Running the emotional gambit of a fight or maybe a break up.

I made it through the Saturday night shows and went to my room. I have so much to do. I start making lists so I don't forget, everything from finding boxes and packing to working on a possible set list for my new show. Danny has called me a few times, but I haven't answered or called back. It really bothered me when he didn't call, but now I don't want to talk to him. It sounds silly, but I don't need the roller coaster ride. Around 2am someone knocks on my door and the first thing I think is "Bryan went back to LA." I peek through the peephole and Tony is standing there. I open the door, "Hey Tony," and gesture inviting him in.

"I'm here on business. I got a call to check on you because you aren't answering your phone."

"Danny is having you check up on me?" Irritation oozes off of me.

"Yes."

"And, I'm guessing he doesn't like that he can't reach me?"

"That would be true."

"What do you think, Tony?"

"I'm staying out of it. Mouth shut. Simply checking to make sure a hotel guest is okay."

"You're a smart man, Tony."

Tony turns to his walkie, "Did you hear that?"

From the walkie I hear Danny, "Yea. Tony, can you help me fix this?"

"No, man. This is outside of my abilities. You'll have to be here to fix this. It's going to take some of your Danny magic and maybe more. I'd be prepared with a back-up plan. By the way, she can hear you."

I stand there glaring at Tony and his walkie, my hip out and tapping my foot. "Are we done here?"

Danny from the walkie, "NO. We're not done. We will never be done. Is she wearing the ring I gave her?"

Tony answers, "Yea, she's still wearing it."

"Good, we're not done. Jacks, please listen to me. I don't know how to make this better, but I'll make it better. I'll try until I figure out what it takes to make you love me again."

"You idiot! I couldn't possibly be this mad at someone

without loving them. I'm pissed off, but I'll always love you."
Boys can be so exasperating.

Tony to his walkie, "Did you catch all that?"

"Yea." Danny actually sounds happy that I'm mad at him. I
hear the relief in his voice, "I love you, Jacks. I think about
you all the time. Please don't be mad."

"Thank you for checking in on me, Tony. Have a good
night," and I shut the door, locking it behind me.

I make it through Sunday unscathed and the week goes
quickly. Dot helps me with packing. I rent a moving truck and
when I leave for Vegas early on Friday morning, my LA apartment is empty. I drive the moving truck with my pickup in tow,
driving toward my dreams and scared of all the change. Dot
promised that I can sleep on her couch whenever I'm in LA,
even when I have to be there for work over the next week or
so. I check in with Katy when I stop to get gas at the state line
to tell her I'm in town and I'll be at my apartment unloading if
she needs me. When I get to my new place the whole stage
crew is there waiting for me, including Katy and the guys. I get
my key from Ron and unlock the door to find the clean empty
space waiting for me. It's perfect. It's home. The stage crew
has already taken the boxes out of my pickup and detached the
tow bar. It makes me happy to know this is going to be a quick
job. I hate moving and I honestly had no idea how I was going
to move my furniture by myself. I turn to Katy, "Thank you for
making this so easy on me."

"Um, I'd love to take credit for it, but it wasn't my idea.
Danny has been calling me to check on you. He asked me to
make sure you had help moving in, even offered to pay guys to
do it for you. I'm not saying you should call him or anything,
but he's a good guy and he misses you." Katy holds her hands
together and smirks.

We start carrying the smaller boxes in while the guys carry
the furniture and set up my bed for me. The moving truck is

completely unloaded, all the furniture is in and all the boxes are stacked neatly in the living room in under two hours. I take everything in, absorbing my new surroundings. It will take me time to make it my place, but I have time to do that. The guys take off, leaving Katy with me. We sort the boxes out by room and arrange the furniture, while we enjoy some girl talk.

CHAPTER THIRTY-ONE

The next month goes by quickly. I'm completely moved in, the cupboards have been lined, my kitchen is organized, my artwork is on the walls, my curtains are up in my bedroom, my stereo is hooked up and it's starting to feel like home. I've been meeting with Ron to prepare for my show and practicing with the Consequences. George has been giving me wardrobe to wear for my show and he's somewhat jealous that I get to wear a wardrobe that's actually me, not tailored to fit the show—the show is tailored to fit me. The MGM has a house hair and make-up person, Marcy and that's short for Marcel. I want to hook him up with George, they'd be great together. Marcy has been great at bringing out my inner rock chick with my make-up and hair, he didn't even complain when I wanted to wear a bandana Axl Rose style—he made it work. Opening night of Jacks! is this Thursday night and I'm beyond excited. The set list is perfect. The band is perfect. I'm featuring Bryan on a couple songs with me during each set, to add some variety. I love it all. But, it's been a lot of work. Long hours of practice and longer sets than I'm accustomed to. My clothes are too big because I'm exuding so much energy on stage and not eating much because nobody's food is Danny's. I'm worn out at the end of the day and sleeping well every night.

I still think about Danny, especially at night when I climb into my bed alone and when there's something that I want to share. But, I haven't called him or talked to him. It may be childish, I just can't. It didn't bother me that he knocked up his co-worker while we were dating, but it was different then. We had already fallen back then, but it wasn't real. I'm not sure if it was my lie or the distance between us, and the time that passed between seeing each other, and I guess it doesn't matter. The fact that we found each other and it was like we could finally breathe again, like life could go back to being in color instead of black and white. The touch that made everything okay and the kiss that made me remember everything we had together like it was yesterday. I'm anxious for the day when that happens again. I hope with all my heart and soul that when that day comes we're stronger for it and this time apart doesn't end us.

We've been through dress rehearsal, my wardrobe is set for opening night and the set is a bit on the fluid side. We decide to go with a list of possible songs and I can call it as I go. There's no curtain at this stage and when I arrive the day of opening night there's a huge neon sign that simply says Jacks! in all caps with kind of a childlike-look hanging over the stage. I absolutely love it and all I can think is that's because of Danny. Admittedly, I'm a bit emotional today with everything going on and it being opening night. I've been in this lounge so many times and everything is fine, but today I remember Ron calling Jess and I out onto the dance floor. I remember Danny dancing with me and it flows into the night Danny brought me back here getting drunk and dancing until Ron told us to get a room. Bryan is on stage and sees me stop as I walk in, "You've got this girl. Keep it together. I'm here and I've got your back," as if he's in my head. I smile at Bryan. It does make this easier having him here.

Katy walks up to me, "Let's go, I'm taking you out to eat. You need food before you do this or you'll waste away to nothing." I let her drag me away. "I took off from the Supper Club today, so I'm here for you until the night is over and then we can go out and celebrate. After all, you're my first client." I hug her, happy that I found her and aware that I couldn't have anybody better looking out for me.

"Thank you. I really need you today." I tell her quietly.

"I had a feeling it might be a hard day. You'll be fine once you're on stage. I can hold you up until then." Lunch was at the MGM spa and included a manicure, pedicure and a body wrap n' scrub treatment for two. I smell like warm vanilla and coconut. It was amazing. Relaxing and rejuvenating at the same time, not to mention that it left my skin glowing.

We go back to the lounge and I get ready for my show. I'm going to say that again, my show. Yeah, too cool. My opening night wardrobe is skintight faded low rider jeans that are ripped in slits across the thighs from seam to seam all the way to my knees, black suede over the knee boots with eight leather belts that wrap around to shiny silver buckles from my ankle to just below my knee, and a metallic dark purple sleeveless, drapey, low cut top. I'm accessorized with a black leather belt low around my hips that has a substantial shiny silver double buckle, bangles the way George always has me wear them, and a long necklace of silver links wrapped around my neck once to fit the base of my neck with an amethyst amulet, and the second loop hanging right down between my breasts. My eyeliner is Vegas heavy and I'm glistening with a light dusting of silver body dust across my collarbone, chest, cheeks, and shoulders. My eye shadow is perfect with smoky lavender highlights. I hear the band on stage and walk to join them before the doors open. "What do you guys think?" I spin around for their approval to a chorus of, "You look great," and "I don't remember you ever looking this good," and, "Let me know if you want to get together later." "Can we get a few songs in before the doors open? I need it."

"You got it," Bryan reads me and starts in on "You Oughta Know," then "Crazy," then "Revolution" by the Beatles, and finally "Piece of My Heart."

The stage crew shut us down and pulled us off stage, so they could open the doors and let in our opening night crowd. The funny thing is that I didn't even think about the fact that we might not have a crowd. I didn't get called on to go out and greet the people waiting to get into the show. I didn't wonder if my friends would show up for opening night. Bryan and the band are here for me. Katy is watching me from just beyond the stage. My show is midweek and it's a Thursday night, anything can happen. Ron's backstage, "You got this, Sweetheart! Go get 'em, Darling." He walks out on stage, takes the mic and says, "Thank you for joining us tonight. This is a big night. I'm happy to see so many of you here on a Thursday. Let me tell you, you're going to love this girl. Now, put your hands together for her first time on stage with her own show and welcome Jacks!"

The applause roars and I walk out on stage. I had no idea there would be so many people waiting for me to take the stage. The room is full and as soon as the sea of people are in my sight, my walk turns into a strut and my smile takes over. I grab the mic from the stand, "Hi everybody. Thanks for coming out. I'm Jacks and these are the Consequences. 1, 2, 3, 4!" and the band starts in on Vixen's "Edge of a Broken Heart." The show leaves me with a stage high unlike any other and the couple of songs with Bryan and his acoustic give me a chance to almost take a break, at least to sit down on a stool while we sing together. Part of the crowd is on their feet for most of the show and at the end we got called out for an encore. We go off the cuff and do Bryan's "That Girl," an old Baby's song "Midnight Rendezvous," and end with "In The End" by the Beatles, but in our slightly harder, updated way. When we're done the stage crew turns the lights down and the place roars. From that point on, my show would always end with that song. It was a rush!

As we walk off the stage Bryan runs up behind me, picks me up and twirls me around, "Wooooo!" For a moment I smile at the contact and enjoy the childlike fun. Our adrenaline is running high from the show. I need that contact after tonight and I'm tempted to take it to another level, the option is there. But, Bryan and I are better as friends. I want him to hit it off with Katy. Mostly, it would only be a one-night stand and cause us trouble on stage. I mean, Bryan already wants to play songs that will take digs at Danny. He'd love it if Danny caught him touching me like this, well until Danny beat the crap out of him. What do I care what Danny thinks? He isn't here and I deserve to be happy.

As I'm having this internal conversation with myself, I watch Bryan walk up to Katy, pick her up and twirl her around. Yea, that's how it's supposed to be. "Hey now, don't make me dizzy," Katy tells him as she leans in and kisses Bryan lightly on the cheek. The shine of her eyes gives away that she's interested in him. Bryan responds by sliding her down his slender body rather than just putting her down, they quickly lock eyes and then look away.

The members of the band high-five me and hug me one by one. Ron walks up to me grinning, "I knew you were good, dear. But, I had no idea of your full potential. You were spectacular."

"Thank you. It really means a lot to me. And Ron, thanks for giving me a chance." I reach up and give him a hug, trying to ignore his old man cologne.

"You owned this stage tonight and you'll just get better.

You should go celebrate with your band. Enjoy it, dear." He pushes me toward the Consequences and Katy.

Something is missing. No, someone is missing. Danny. I let go of my stubborn anger in hopes of being happy and call Danny. The phone rings, and rings, but nobody answers it. I deserve that. Katy grabs me, "Let's get you drunk," and I let her.

CHAPTER THIRTY-TWO

The weekend sets at the Supper Club go well and I've been spending time with the vocalists, helping them get better. But, I can't wait for Monday. Now that I've done my show, I want to do it again and I want to do it better. The Archies are great, but something about the Consequences makes it for me. Maybe it's the familiarity, our history, Bryan, or the fact that we're in tune on what style music we want to play.

I have practice with the Consequences on Monday in the early afternoon and we run through the songs we performed on opening night, talking about what went well, what could be better, what was missing and what needs to go. We all agree that we like ending with "In the End" and play it a few times to get the harder version of it where we want it. I want to add a couple of ballads or love songs to the set. I keep coming back to Foreigner's "Waiting For a Girl Like You," but I opt for "I Want To Know What Love Is." We play through both a couple times and either are possibilities. Bryan suggests something classic and powerful to balance everything out, he wants to add a Led Zeppelin tune to the set. "Bry, I've never got the Led out." He insists that it's time that I try and the band starts in on the hard driving "Immigrant Song." I make it through good, but I need practice on the lyrics and the timing. I get the guys to humor me with some White Lion and we agree on Kix's "Don't Close Your Eyes" for a little bit of darkness. In reality, we're increasing our list of possibilities and reorganizing until we get it right. We break and find food before the show.

There's been nothing from Danny and since I'm not staying at the Stardust any more, Tony hasn't checked in on me.

Another week goes by and my show is getting better. I'm quickly getting noticed on the Vegas scene. Women are coming to my show wanting the band, and guys are hitting on me, leaving me their phone number, bringing me flowers, reaching for me while I'm on stage—some even waiting at the exit for us to leave the lounge. Bryan is ignoring all of it and focusing on music, I'd bet he's writing. But the rest of the Consequences are loving the attention. It's all part of the gig, keep the people happy. So I smile and choose guys in the audience to sing to, connect with, flirt with, and have fun. But only from the safety of the stage.

A couple of weeks later we have fine-tuned to three different sets with a couple songs we switch in and out. There's been a line three hours early to get in for my show and it's been filling up pretty consistently. I'd guess it's mostly locals mid-week, and I'm not complaining about the local following. Katy has been bringing me food and taking me out to eat because I continue to lose weight with my performance schedule, and as she likes to remind me that I haven't been eating. She's worried about me, but I'm a big girl. She's even got Bryan forcing snacks on me.

Katy is at the MGM backstage with me one Tuesday night, nothing out of the ordinary since she's usually here when the Supper Club is dark. The stage is dark and the doors open, the crowd pours in and that means we have about twenty minutes before the show starts. Most of these people have been waiting at least an hour. The cocktail waitresses make their way through the crowds providing the cure to help them all relax. The doors shut because we're at capacity and I'm warming up, jumping around a little to stay pumped up, singing "You Oughta Know" backstage and playing with the band members. The house crew pulls Katy away and the lights go up before she gets back. I'm ready to rock it tonight and may even debut my Led Zeppelin song. We start the set with my Vixen tune and I survey the room to find out who's here tonight, connecting with the crowd. Katy's walking across the back of the room. Odd because she's always back-stage. The only time she's on the floor is during practice. I turn to Bryan for an answer, but he shrugs his shoulders. Then Katy walks back through, leading someone through the crowd to the backstage. This fucking hot guy with shaggy blonde hair, wearing a tight black T-shirt and Levi's. Bryan gives me a questioning stare, wondering why Katy has a dude with her but doesn't worry about it when he sees the expression on my face as I realize it's Danny. I take the mic off the stand, "Welcome everybody, thanks for coming out tonight. I've got someone special in the building for the first time tonight, so indulge me if I change up the set a bit. By the way, I'm Jacks and these are the Consequences." I turn to Bryan for approval and get a nod. We play "Cryin'" by Aerosmith, followed by "I Want To Know What Love Is" by Foreigner and "Always" by Bon Jovi. The emotion of it takes everything out of me and tears are rolling down my face. I'm suddenly exhausted, but I can't stop. I'm driven to put it all out there. I don't know any other way than putting my whole heart into everything. Danny walks out on the stage to me quickly as "Always" comes to an end and Bryan meets him there taking the mic from my hand. I collapse into Danny's arms and he carries me off stage.

Bryan covers, playing a couple originals by the Consequences.

Danny holds me to him, "I've got you, baby. I love you, Jacks. I'm not leaving again." I realize he's the only thing keeping me standing. Katy starts pouring water into me and forcing food on me. "Why didn't you tell me?" Danny asks Katy.

"Not my place. We've been doing the best we can to get her to eat. I think having you show up was too much." Katy really has been taking care of me more than I was aware.

I get my legs back and try to break away for the stage. I have to get back out there. Danny won't let me go. "I'm going back out there, so let me go or go with me." He follows me out and moves the stool over, Bryan follows suit and grabs his stool for our acoustic songs. Danny leaves me once I'm sitting and Bryan starts in on "To Be With You" by Mr. Big, then "High Enough" by Damn Yankees. Bryan turns to Katy for direction and gets a nod. He takes control of the set and keeps the acoustic songs going with some back up from the rest of the band, going with "Love of a Lifetime" by Firehouse, then "Signs" by Tesla and Skid Row's "I Remember You." I stand up and kick the stool away for Skid Row and the band comes in full force, Bryan goes along with it even though he isn't sure and stays close to me. Danny is ready to come out and get me, but Katy holds him back. We make it through the show and take longer than we should before we go back on stage for our encore. Bryan already did "That Girl," so I go with "Waiting For a Girl Like You" by Foreigner, then we string together "If I Fell," "And I Love Her," "We Can Work It Out" and "In My Life" before "In the End." The crowd goes crazy when the lights go down. Danny is waiting for me, watching the band and I as we hug and high-five. Watching Bryan as he picks me up and twirls me around on his way off the stage, just like every night and then moves to Katy doing the same thing, but claims her mouth with his as he slides her down his body.

I walk up to Danny, "Hey stranger."

Danny puts his arms around me, "Jacks, you need to eat. You're so skinny."

"Then you'll have to cook for me, because nothing else is any good." Danny laughs and puts his forehead against mine.

"You got it, babe. Right now. Jacks, you have me for two weeks."

"You said you weren't leaving again," I stare at him beginning to feel the hurt again.

"I'm not leaving, I meant you have me to yourself for two weeks. My mom has Jackie and I'm not going back to work for two weeks. I need to find a new place and get moved in before mom gets here with Jackie. Mom is moving here to watch Jackie while we get settled, to give us more time together and ease the transition. I'm hoping she likes it and will stay in Vegas."

I look at him lost. "We get two weeks together?"

Danny smiles, "We get forever together, Jacks. I'll be with you every night and be there when you wake up every morning, if you'll have me." Danny kneels down and gazes up at me while he holds my left hand taking off my champagne cage ring and replacing it with a diamond.

EPILOGUE

I pull Danny up off his knee and kiss him. "I don't understand." I focus on him searching for answers.

"Jacks, someday is here. She's gone. We have nothing to hide. I don't want you to be a secret, you never deserved that. I want to be with you forever and I'm hoping," Danny looks down and takes a deep breath, "Begging you to be with me, keep me, and I come packaged with Jackie. Please, my Jacks." He slides his foot across the floor waiting for a response and not able to handle the silence, "I know that I haven't always made the best choices and I've done some stupid things. I'm working on that and I promise that I'll never leave you for any reason. Please let me love you. Give me a…"

I cut him off, "Danny, sshhhhh." I hold my finger to his lips. I'm shocked at the idea of our someday being real and being now. "Is it really our someday? Nothing to keep us apart?" Danny nods. My face lights up, warming my cheeks. "We get to be together even in public?" Danny nods. "You want to marry me?"

"Yes, Jacks. I want to marry you."

"We get to live together?"

"Yes, babe. And, I'm hoping you're up for my instant daughter package. The three of us together as a family." Danny waits for me to do something other than ask a question.

"Danny, there's nothing I want more. But," I watch Danny get that oh shit what expression on his face and start to turn white, "Tonight can I just have you?"

"You get just me for two weeks and mom is going to babysit for us after that. She wants us happy. That ring was my grandmother's." Danny pulls me close and puts his forehead to mine, "So, give me a yes and make me know you want to marry me please."

I was so shook up by everything that had happened, I didn't respond. I get my head straight after sorting it out in my head. "Yes! Danny, of course yes!" I reach my arms around his neck, jump up wrapping my legs around his waist and kiss him until I'm dizzy. I lay my head on his shoulder and Danny walks to Katy.

"Katy, I'm taking my fiancé home to cook for her now."

Katy shakes her head at us and smiles, "It's about time. I'm cancelling tomorrow's practice. She needs to be here by 5pm tomorrow for the show. Have fun." She gestures with her hand shooing us away.

We walk out to my pickup in the parking lot. Danny still carrying me, he pins me against my truck. He kisses me desperately like he needs my kiss to breathe and I feel the same way. It's like my heart finally starts beating again. All the shades of gray that have been hovering over me are gone, cleared away by technicolor dreams coming true. He puts me in the passenger side and drives us home, as I give him directions to my apartment.

We get home and he sits me on the kitchen counter as he searches my cabinets and refrigerator, trying to find supplies, tools, food to work with and get me fed. My kitchen is small and barely counts as a kitchen. He digs in the refrigerator and pantry finding something to work with and looks at me, "Tomorrow we're going grocery shopping. I think I can make something work." Danny gets some pasta boiling and makes a cheese sauce with whatever cheese I had in the refrigerator. He tosses frozen veggies in the microwave and glares at me disturbed by frozen produce. Magically making pasta with veggies in cheese sauce. "I'm not happy with this, but it's what's available." While I eat he mixes up a quick batter and divides it into a few small dishes, then puts them in the microwave. "Tell me what you think of this," he says as he sets one of the dishes from the microwave in front of me with a scoop of chocolate chip ice cream on top of it. It smells amazing and the ice cream is melting as I dig into it, oh man… peanut butter cake. "Good, that's what I want to hear," and Danny smiles at me. I realize I must've made sex noises again at the taste of the dessert. He sits there watching me and hands me another dish of the pasta.

I look up at him stuffed, "I'm full."

"Okay, you can have more later. You need to eat." Danny's concerned, "I'm sorry. I didn't know how hard this was on you."

I set the dessert aside and reach for him, "None of it matters. I have you now." Danny gazes into my eyes and puts his lips on mine, doing his Danny thing as he moves his tongue across my lips to have me open for him. I encourage him further and he carries me to the bedroom, treating me like a fragile piece of art. He turns the blankets down and sets me on the bed. I need him badly. I need to feel him against me. I need to feel him inside me. I need to move with him. He watches me with a funny look on his face as I pull off my boots and strip quickly.

"Babe, you need rest."

I reach for him and unbutton his fly, rubbing him through his jeans in the process. "I've had too many nights of sleep alone. I need you more than I need to rest. We can sleep later. Besides, you promised that you would be with me when I wake up everyday." I push his Levi's down enough to release Tiger.

"I did. I will." Danny focuses on me in a new way. Maybe everything suddenly hit him. Maybe he finally realized we're really getting our someday. Maybe it hit him that we're engaged, or maybe he counted the days since we had sex. I can tell you the number of days, too many. I hit the remote for my stereo and turn on the Vegas hard rock station.

He's trying to do what he thinks is the right thing, trying to hold back. "Danny, I'm okay. You don't need to hold back. You need to make me yours. Now, please take your shirt off so I can examine that sexy tattoo and love me like only you can." I grin at him with a giggle. He strips completely and climbs in bed with me, pulling the blankets up over us like a fort.

He wraps his arms around me, holding me tight and kissing my forehead. "I love you, Jacks. I missed you so much. I just want to hold you." I reach for Tiger, running my finger along his hard long length and his body wants to do more than hold me. I grind my naked body against him and draw a manly sound from him. I push him to his back and climb on top of him, lying on him with my head on his shoulder. He strokes my back lovingly and continues to hold me. I squeeze Tiger with my thighs and wriggle around a bit. "Jacks, you're playing dirty." I feel Tiger searching for my entrance and help him, rubbing my wet heat on him. I slide down getting the tip inside me and slowly sit up as he fills me.

I'm transported away, "I need this. I need you, Danny. I need to feel you and move with you. Only you, baby." Moving to get him as deep as I can, taking him further and further as

I'm able. "You're amazing, Danny." I lean forward and reach to kiss him, stroking him with my tight sex and drawing a curse from his lips. But, he's right and I don't have the energy. "Please take me, Danny."

He pulls me to his chest and holds me, cherishing me. Then he rolls me under him and my body begins to sing in joy of what is coming next. "I love you, Jacks... no marathons tonight. I do need to have you..." he trails off as he pushes into me, "fuck me, you're like a glove." He pushes in more and pulls out slowly, moving deliberately, feeling me and driving me crazy with heat. He kisses my neck with his open mouth, slowly and hot with his tongue. His breath at my ear making me want more and leading me with his words. "Baby, I missed this so much. Nobody feels like you. I swear you were made for me, you're so fucking perfect. I'm a dumb man for waiting so long to make you mine. I never should've let you go the first time." His intensity growing with his words, moving faster and harder. He's getting close. "Tell me..." I lose him again.

"You're so hard, oh Danny! More baby. I'm yours, baby. Only us," he has me screaming out with every stroke and I can't control myself. I'm on fire and I wrap my legs around him, meeting his every stroke.

"Oh, baby... with me." He's breathing ragged and out of control. I pull his mouth to mine, needing his kiss and he sucks on my tongue. Our bodies writhing together with need, both of us crying out. He pounds into me hard and sends me over the edge. Flashes of light explode behind my closed eyelids and he changes his pace, slowing back to his deliberate pace, building the friction, pushing my orgasm to keep rolling. I reach for him, wanting my hands on whatever part of him that I can get as I call out his name. "Mmmmm.." Is all that comes from Danny, he loves the feel of me going off around him. He can't help himself and he strokes into me faster, sending himself to climax. He collapses on me and wraps his arms around me with his mouth at my ear, "Only us, Jacks. Always."

I wake up the next morning with Danny's arms around me and using him as my pillow, our legs entangled.

I know it's the beginning, but there's nothing in our way.

FOR ONE LASS

Naomi Springthorp

From Storybook Pub: A Contemporary Romance Collection

When you take a vacation, you should vacate. Sometimes I think I take it a bit too far, but what would life be without experience? For some, the getaway may be a tropical island or an exotic rainforest. For others, a ritzy hotel surrounded by culture. For me, it was simply walking into the Storybook Pub.

I don't know what I was doing there. I had to get out and went for a walk. My life had become mundane. I was bored with it and my circumstances weren't going to change. I'd never been one to run from my responsibilities and commitments, simply vacate them temporarily. Nobody needed to know.

It was a dreary night and the rain began to pour. I didn't turn back. I moved forward and ducked under an awning to escape the rain. I stood there watching the rain fall heavier from the sky when the clouds opened with a roar of thunder. Chilled by the dark wet night that continued to get wetter, warmth and light from the establishment lending me its awning was inviting. I tucked myself into a dry corner and gazed through the window observing the patrons of the Irish pub. I was drawn in by the warmth shining through the window of the Storybook Pub. Odd that I'd walked here hundreds of times yet never saw the establishment before. It's as if it appeared out of nowhere to invite me in for the night, and I didn't turn it down.

The patrons were all in groups, partying to their hearts content. The servers were everyone's friends yet moved with clockwork efficiency. The barkeep was telling a never-ending story to whoever would listen, as he filled glasses up and down the bar. I sat off to the side and watched it all over the top of my menu. Chilled, I reviewed the drink menu with house cocktails, Irish beer, and ciders. The servers were all young ladies wearing tight jeans and dress shirts unbuttoned to show off their cleavage. I'd seen worse and imagined it helped with their tips.

The Dark

I'd started to read the storybook left on the table when he walked up to me and spoke in his Irish accent, "Welcome. Would you like to order or just getting out of the rain tonight?" Where the gorgeous man came from, I have no idea. He simply appeared like the pub in the first place. His presence made my belly flutter before he said a single word. His sexy unkempt jet-black hair hung into his face like a shield for his eyes. But, not enough to hide his piercing ice blues. He was tall and slender with very little fat on his body, if any at all. The closer I looked the more I saw and my intrigue grew. Tentacles of tattoos reached out of his long sleeves, as well as up his neck to the underside of his chin. I wondered where else they went and if he was completely covered.

ACKNOWLEDGMENTS

My world has been turned into a beautiful chaos over the last year. Thanks to the support of my readers, friends, and Love & Devotion family I've finally managed to get Jacks complete. Thank you to all of you for your patience.

A special thank you to Sara "Queen Bee" Cunningham for staying on my case and holding me accountable—its not easy to help a Leo.

There wouldn't be a Love & Devotion without Tonya Clark. She listens to my crazy ideas and says, "okay." It's how we get in trouble. It's how I've somehow become a model hunter or oiler (as Tonya likes to say). It's why we're organizing author events and making bigger plans for 2021 even though the pandemic has screwed up 2020. It's why we have committed to release at least 9 more anthologies before the end of 2022. It's why I'm proud to say this is the first novel to be published by Love & Devotion Author Services, Inc. Thank you to my partner in crime.

ABOUT THE AUTHOR

USA Today Bestselling Author Naomi Springthorp is a born and raised Southern California girl. She's a baseball freak who supports her team all season long and blatantly admires the athletes in those pants. Music has always been part of her life and she believes everything has a soundtrack. She loves her two feline fur babies, though they're not quite sure what to do with her.

She writes Baseball Romance, Romantic Comedies, 90s Throwback, and Contemporary Romance--all with heat and sometimes a little sweet.

Join her newsletter at
www.naomispringthorp.com/sign-up

[f] facebook.com/naomithewriter

[twitter] twitter.com/naomithewriter

[instagram] instagram.com/naomispringthorp

[g] goodreads.com/naomithewriter

[a] amazon.com/author/naomispringthorp

[BB] bookbub.com/authors/naomi-springthorp

ALSO BY NAOMI SPRINGTHORP

AN ALL ABOUT THE DIAMOND ROMANCE

The Sweet Spot

King of Diamonds

Diamonds in Paradise

Star-Crossed in the Outfield

The Closer

Falling for Prince

Up to Bat

BETTING ON LOVE

Just a California Girl

Jacks

Strings Attached

STANDALONE NOVELS & NOVELLAS

Muffin Man

Finally in Focus

Confessions of an Online Junkie

ANTHOLOGIES & BOX SETS

Sacrifice for Love

Storybook Pub

Storybook Pub Christmas Wishes

Young Crush

Storybook Pub 2

Hate to Want You

Tricks, Treats, & Teasers

Caught Under the Mistletoe

All Access Pass

LOVE & DEVOTION AUTHOR SERVICES, INC.

Book Signing Events, Anthologies, Author Services, & more!

Anthologies
Storybook Pub
Storybook Pub Christmas Wishes
Storybook Pub 2
Young Crush
Tricks, Treats, & Teasers
Caught Under the Mistletoe

Sign up for our newsletter at:
www.lovedevotionevents.com

Join us at:
www.facebook.com/groups/lovedevotionevents

facebook.com/lovedevotionevents
twitter.com/lovedevotionae
instagram.com/lovedevotionevents

Made in the USA
Columbia, SC
27 June 2023

19416290R00138